Science 4 Today

Grade 5

by
Margaret Fetty

Frank Schaffer Publications®

Author: Margaret Fetty
Editor: Nathan Hemmelgarn

Frank Schaffer Publications®

Send all inquiries to:
Frank Schaffer Publications
Orion Place
Columbus, Ohio 43240-2111

4 Today—grade 5

682-3525-1

1 2 3 4 5 6 7 8 9 10 POH 12 11 10 09 08 07

Table of Contents

Science and Technology

Science in Personal and Social Perspectives

History and the Nature of Science

What Is Science 4 Today?

Science 4 Today is a comprehensive yet quick and easy-to-use supplement designed to complement any science curriculum. Based on the National Science Education Standards (NSES), forty topics cover essential concepts that fifth-grade students should understand and know in natural science. During the course of four days, presumably Monday through Thursday, students complete questions and activities focusing on each topic in about ten minutes. On the fifth day, students complete a twenty-minute assessment to practice test-taking skills, including multiple choice, true-false, and short answer.

How Does It work?

Unlike many science programs, *Science 4 Today* adopts the eight major standards outlined by the NSES to ascertain students' science skills. The standards are:

- unifying concepts and processes in science.
- science as inquiry.
- physical science.
- life science.
- Earth and space science.
- science and technology.
- science in personal and social perspectives.
- history and nature of science.

The book supplies forty topics commonly found in the fifth-grade science curriculum. Educators can choose a topic confident that it will support their unit of study and at least one of the eight standards. The Skills and Concepts chart on pages 8–10 identifies the main concepts for each week to insure that the content aligns with the classroom topic. The Scope and Sequence chart further supports identifying the specific skills following the standards. The answer key, found on pages 93–112, is provided for both daily activities and general assessments.

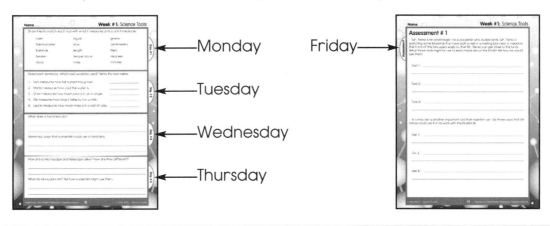

Monday

Tuesday

Wednesday

Thursday

Friday

How Was It Developed?

Science 4 Today was created in response to a need to assess students' understanding of important science concepts. Basals teach the necessary skills, but might not apply them to other overarching standards outlined by the NSES. Moreover, with the increased emphasis on standardized testing, the necessity for experience with test styles and semantics also becomes apparent.

How Can It Be Used?

Science 4 Today can be easily implemented into the daily routine of the classroom, depending on your teaching style. The activities and questions can be written on the board each day, or the whole page can be copied on a transparency and displayed at the appropriate time. It is also possible to copy the weekly page as a blackline master and distribute it at the beginning of each week. Students can complete the activities during attendance or other designated time. After completion, the class can briefly check and discuss the assignment.

What Are the Benefits?

The daily approach of *Science 4 Today* provides reading comprehension practice in science, higher-level thinking exercises, and problem-solving strategies. The pages also target test-taking skills by incorporating the style and syntax of standardized tests. Because of its consistent format, *Science 4 Today* not only offers opportunities for instruction but also serves as an excellent diagnostic tool.

Test-Taking Tips

Short Answer Questions

- Read the directions carefully. Be sure you know what you are expected to do. Ask questions if you do not understand.

- Read the whole question before you answer it. Some questions might have multiple parts.

- If you do not know the answer right away, come back to it after completing the other items.

- Review each question and answer after completing the whole test. Does your answer make sense? Does it answer the whole question?

- Check for spelling, punctuation, and grammar mistakes.

Multiple Choice Questions

- Read the question before looking at the answers. Then, come up with the answer in your head before looking at the choices to avoid confusion.

- Read all the answers before choosing the best answer.

- Eliminate answers that you know are not correct.

- Fill in the whole circle. Do not mark outside the circle.

- Review the questions and your answers after completing the whole test. Your first response is usually correct unless you did not read the question correctly.

True – False Questions

- Read each statement carefully. Look at the key words to understand the statement.

- Look at the qualifying words. Words like *all, always*, and *never* often signal a false statement. General words, like *sometimes, often*, and *usually*, most likely signal a true statement.

- If any part of the statement is false, the whole statement is false.

Skills and Concepts

Science as Inquiry
Week 1 - Pages 13 and 14
The Science Process Skills
process skills
variable
measurement

Week 2 - Pages 15 and 16
From Hypothesis to Law
scientific method
hypothesis
theory
law

Week 3 - Pages 17 and 18
Measuring and Graphic Aids
customary system
metric system
graphic aid
data

Week 4 - Pages 19 and 20
Experiments
experiment
controlled

Week 5 - Pages 21 and 22
A Good Scientist
characteristics
communication

Physical Science
Week 6 - Pages 23 and 24
Elements
atoms
electron
proton
neutron
nucleus
periodic table
atomic number

Week 7 - Pages 25 and 26
Properties of Matter
molecule
compound

mixture
solution
property
physical change
chemical change

Week 8 - Pages 27 and 28
Motion
Speed
inertia
gravity
friction

Week 9 - Pages 29 and 30
Energy
thermal energy
mechanical energy
electrical energy
chemical energy
radiant energy
kinetic energy
potential energy

Week 10 - Pages 31 and 32
Electricity
charges
circuit
generator
turbine
electromagnet

Week 11 - Pages 33 and 34
Sound
vibrations
wavelength
frequency
pitch

Life Science
Week 12 - Pages 35 and 36
Classifying
scientific classification
scientific name
kingdom
genus
species

Week 13 - Pages 37 and 38
Cells

Scope and Sequence

Skills/Concepts	1	2	3	4	5	6	7	8	9	10	11	12	13	14	15	16	17	18	19	20	21	22	23	24	25	26	27	28	29	30	31	32	33	34	35	36	37	38	39	40
Unifying Concepts and Processes in Science																																								
Systems			•										•																•										•	
Order and organization		•										•	•	•		•													•					•				•	•	
Measuring			•							•												•																		
Science as Inquiry																																								
Science process skills	•			•											•		•		•		•	•			•	•	•								•	•				•
Scientific method	•	•		•														•					•		•				•			•					•			
Science inquiry			•	•																			•			•									•	•	•	•		
Physical Science																																								
Elements						•			•	•													•														•			
Properties of matter							•		•	•													•		•	•											•			
Motion								•										•					•				•								•		•			
Energy									•											•					•	•	•									•	•			
Properties of electricity										•																														
Properties of sound											•																										•			
Life Science																																								
Classifying												•	•	•	•																•									
Cells																													•		•								•	
Heredity and reproduction														•	•																•								•	
Adaptations															•																									
Energy in Ecosystems																•																		•					•	
Populations																	•																•							
Earth and Space Science																																								
Earth's layers																		•																				•		
Resources																			•															•	•	•				

• Indicates Skill or Concept Included

Scope and Sequence

Skills/Concepts	1	2	3	4	5	6	7	8	9	10	11	12	13	14	15	16	17	18	19	20	21	22	23	24	25	26	27	28	29	30	31	32	33	34	35	36	37	38	39	40
Changes on Earth																				•		•						•												
Atmosphere																					•						•	•					•							
Climate																						•						•												
Solar system																							•				•	•							•		•		•	
Science and Technology																																								
Computers																								•		•														
NASA's contributions																									•															
Medical technology																										•														
Telescopes																											•													
Satellites																												•												
Science in Personal and Social Perspectives																																								
Body systems																													•	•										
Healthy lifestyles																														•	•				•					
Diseases																															•									
Pollution																																•								
Human impact																																•	•	•						
Solid wastes																																•		•						
History and Nature of Science																																								
Egyptian contributions																																			•					
Automobiles																																				•				
Sir Isaac Newton																												•									•			
Fossils																																						•		
Cycles																•	•	•				•																	•	
Kid inventors																																							•

• Indicates Skill or Concept Included

Draw a line to match each science process skill with its definition.

observing   grouping objects based on characteristics or qualities

classifying   using your five senses to learn about the world

communicating   telling how objects are alike and different

inferring   using what you know to make a guess about what will happen

predicting   sharing information using words, charts, diagrams, and graphs

comparing   using what you know and what you learn to make conclusions

Day #1

Give an example of how you could use each science process skill.

making and using models: _____

_____

making operational definitions: _____

_____

Day #2

What is a variable?

_____

_____

Why would a scientist need to identify and control variables in an experiment?

_____

_____

Day #3

Name two reasons that scientists make measurements.

_____

_____

Why might a scientist estimate a measurement?

_____

_____

Day #4

Assessment # 1

Read the paragraph. Then, answer the questions.

Dan takes a magnet off the refrigerator and experiments with its magnetic force. He finds that it is attracted to silverware, a lamp base, a metal bowl, but not the front of the dishwasher. He thinks it will be attracted to the handle on the back door. When Dan tests his idea, he finds that not only does it stick to the handle, but it sticks to the door, as well. He concludes that the door is metal.

1. Identify and explain three science process skills that Dan uses.

_____

_____

_____

2. What operational definition could Dan make for the word *magnet*?

_____

_____

3. How did Dan identify and control variables?

_____

_____

Fill in the circle next to the best answer.

4. Dan sorts the objects into two groups—those that are attracted to the magnet and those that are not. Which science process skill did Dan use?

(A) interpreting data   (C) estimating

(B) classifying   (D) predicting

5. What would be the best way for Dan to communicate his findings?

(A) chart   (C) bar graph

(B) line graph   (D) diagram

Write numbers **1** through **8** to show the steps of the scientific method.

_____ Interpret the data

_____ Investigate further

_____ Plan the experiment and the variables

_____ State the problem

_____ Test the hypothesis

_____ Collect the data

_____ Communicate the conclusion

_____ Formulate a hypothesis

What is a hypothesis?

_____

Circle the best hypothesis.

Will a wagon move more easily over rocks or concrete?

A rock driveway is better than a concrete driveway.

A wagon will move more easily over a concrete driveway than a rock driveway.

Name two reasons telling why scientists follow the scientific method.

_____

_____

_____

Why do scientists communicate information about their experiments?

_____

_____

What is a theory?

_____

_____

How is a theory different from a law?

_____

_____

Assessment

Assessment # 2

Answer the questions.

1. What is the correct order in the scientific process? Write numbers **1** through **5**.

_____ theory

_____ hypothesis

_____ question

_____ law

_____ experiment

2. Why does it take so long for scientists to agree on a scientific law?

_____

_____

3. Read the statement below. Identify what part of the scientific process it is. Explain how you know.

An object will remain in motion or stay at rest until a force acts on it.

_____

_____

Fill in the circle next to the best answer.

4. What will a scientist most likely do if the hypothesis and conclusion do not match?

(A) Identify the hypothesis as a theory.

(B) Communicate the results with the scientific community.

(C) State a new hypothesis.

(D) Give up because the hypothesis was wrong.

5. Which of the activities will a scientist not do during an experiment?

(A) follow a set of steps   (C) change one variable

(B) observe the action   (D) explain the action

What is the customary system of measurement?

_____

_____

What is the metric system of measurement?

_____

_____

Day #1

What measurement system is used in the science community?

_____

Why do all scientists use this system?

_____

_____

_____

Day #2

Mia made a chart to show the kinds of materials in her recycling bin. What two conclusions can she make based on the data in the chart?

Material	Number of Pieces
aluminum	8
tin	2
plastics	3
glass	2
paper	5

_____

_____

_____

_____

Day #3

Draw a graphic aid to show the data in the chart above.

Day #4

Assessment # 3

Complete the page.

For an experiment, Carla grew a plant. She measured its growth each week and recorded the data in a chart.

Week	Height (cm)
1	0.5
2	1.0
3	1.5
4	2.0
5	3.0
6	5.0
7	7.0
8	9.0

1. Draw a line graph to show the data.

2. Why is a line graph the best graphic aid to show the data?

_____

_____

Fill in the circle next to the best answer.

3. If the trend continues, what will be the height of the plant on Week 10?

(A) 10 cm   (C) 13 cm

(B) 11 cm   (D) 20 cm

Name

Write *true* or *false*.

1. _____ An experiment always tests a hypothesis.
2. _____ A scientist makes a prediction based on the results of the experiment.
3. _____ Experiments need to be controlled to make sure they are fair.
4. _____ It is important to change at least two variables during an experiment.
5. _____ All data needs to be carefully recorded during an experiment.

Should you read through the entire set of instructions before beginning an experiment? Explain.

_____

_____

_____

_____

_____

What are three kinds of clothing people can wear to protect themselves during an experiment?

_____

_____

What are three kinds of clothing people should not wear while performing an experiment?

_____

_____

What are three safety rules, not related to clothing, that people should follow during an experiment?

_____

_____

_____

_____

Assessment # 4

Complete the page.

1. Lana noticed that some plants in the backyard were turning yellow. What should Lana do before stating a hypothesis?

_____

_____

_____

_____

2. In planning the experiment, what three materials might Lana need?

_____

_____

_____

3. Describe an experiment Lana can do to find out why the plants are turning yellow.

_____

_____

_____

_____

_____

_____

_____

_____

Week #5: A Good Scientist

Scientists have certain characteristics that help them do their best work. Write **C** in front of each characteristic that you think is important for a scientist to have.

_____ curious   _____ patient   _____ creative

_____ observant   _____ speedy   _____ uninterested

_____ careless   _____ eager   _____ persistent

Choose two characteristics. Tell why they are important qualities for a scientist to have.

_____

_____

Day #1

Communication is another characteristic important in a scientist. Why do scientists need to communicate?

_____

_____

Name three ways that a scientist might communicate.

_____

_____

Day #2

Name two reasons why a good scientist takes careful notes?

_____

_____

_____

_____

_____

Day #3

Think about your characteristics. Would you make a good scientist? Explain. Give two examples to support your opinion.

_____

_____

_____

_____

_____

Day #4

Assessment

Assessment # 5

Read the paragraph. Then, answer the question.

Beatrix Potter is best known for writing and illustrating *The Tale of Peter Rabbit*. However, she was also a mycologist, a person who studies fungi. Potter collected samples of many different fungi and then dissected them to see what they looked like inside. Afterward, she would paint detailed illustrations showing what they looked like. Potter painted nearly 300 pictures of mushrooms. She submitted a paper to a science society telling of some of her discoveries. However, it was not accepted.

1. Why was Beatrix Potter a good scientist? Write a paragraph explaining three characteristics.

_____

_____

_____

_____

_____

_____

Fill in the circle next to the best answer.

2. What will a good scientist do?

   (A) take careful notes

   (B) conduct one experiment to prove a hypothesis

   (C) record data at the end of an experiment

   (D) share the data that supports his hypothesis

3. How does data help a scientist?

   (A) It shows the scientist conducted an experiment.

   (B) It proves the scientist's ideas are valid.

   (C) It explains the steps in the experiment.

   (D) It helps the scientist make a hypothesis.

Write a word to correctly complete each sentence.

1. _____ is anything that has mass and takes up space.

2. An _____ is the building block of matter.

3. The smallest particle of matter is an _____.

4. The _____ table lists all the elements.

Write *true* or *false*.

1. _____ There are about 100 elements.

2. _____ Heat and light can break down elements.

3. _____ Elements can be combined to make different kinds of matter.

4. _____ Most elements are nonmetal.

5. _____ A period table groups elements by their properties and atomic number.

Label the atom.

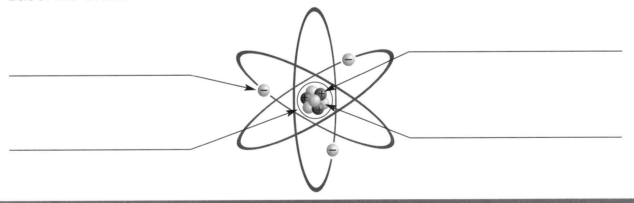

Look at the element from the periodic table. Then, answer the questions.

8
O

1. What is the name of this element? _____

2. What does the atomic number tell? _____

3. How many electrons does this element have? _____

4. What does the letter **O** represent? _____

Assessment # 6

Fill in the circle next to the best answer.

1. Which is not an element?

   (A) silver   (C) iron

   (B) water   (D) aluminum

2. How are elements arranged in the periodic table?

   (A) by the mass of the nucleus

   (B) in alphabetical order

   (C) in the order they were discovered

   (D) by the number of protons

Answer the questions.

3. Describe the particles in an atom and their charges.

   _____

   _____

   _____

4. If an atomic number for an element is 15, what two facts do you know?

   _____

   _____

   _____

5. Why are elements called the *building blocks of matter*?

   _____

   _____

   _____

What is a molecule?

_____

_____

How are molecules similiar to atoms?

_____

_____

What is a compound?

_____

_____

Give an example of a compound. Identify its parts.

_____

_____

How is a mixture the same as and different from a solution?

_____

_____

_____

Is saltwater a mixture or a solution? Explain.

_____

_____

Write **P** in front of each physical change. Write **C** in front of each chemical change.

_____ cut   _____ tear   _____ melt

_____ grind   _____ bake   _____ rust

_____ burn   _____ tarnish   _____ digestion

Assessment

Assessment # 7

Answer the questions.

1. A green banana turns yellow as it ripens. What kind of change is taking place?

_____

_____

2. What are three physical properties of iron? What is a chemical property of iron?

_____

_____

3. What are two ways to separate a compound?

_____

_____

4. Give an example of a mixture. Explain how you know that it is a mixture.

_____

_____

Fill in the circle next to the best answer.

5. What is lemonade?

   (A) a molecule   (C) an element

   (B) a compound   (D) a solution

6. Which is not a physical property?

   (A) color   (C) elasticity

   (B) texture   (D) reacts to heat

What is speed?

_____

_____

Mrs. Carlos drives 150 kilometers in 2 hours. What is her speed per hour? Explain how you found the answer.

_____

_____

Write a word to complete each sentence.

1. The tendency for an object to stay at rest or in motion is called

    _____.

2. A _____ can make something move or cause it to stop.

3. The pull of _____ is weaker when two objects are farther apart.

4. The measure of speed in a certain direction is called _____.

5. When a car _____, its rate of speed changes.

Think about riding in a car. What happens to your body when the car stops suddenly? Explain what force is at work.

_____

_____

How does an object's mass affect its motion?

_____

_____

_____

What is friction?

_____

_____

What are three ways to reduce friction?

_____

_____

Assessment

Assessment # 8

Answer the questions.

1. Why would you weigh less on the moon?

_____

_____

_____

2. Think about kicking a soccer ball into a goal. It flies into the air, drops into the goal, and rolls to a stop. Describe three forces that affect the ball's movement.

_____

_____

_____

Fill in the circle next to the best answer.

3. Ada was walking north. She turned left and started walking west. What did Ada change?

(A) speed   (C) inertia

(B) velocity   (D) acceleration

4. What happens when two balls of different masses are dropped from the same height?

(A) Gravity pulls them close together.

(B) Their speed is different.

(C) The larger ball hits the ground first.

(D) Their acceleration is the same.

5. Which surface provides the greatest amount of friction?

(A) ice   (C) grass

(B) pebbles   (D) concrete

Draw a line to match each term with its meaning.

thermal energy   the energy that is stored and released by changes in the connection of atoms

mechanical energy   the energy that travels as waves and through empty space

electrical energy   the energy an object has because it can move or is moving

chemical energy   the energy caused by the flow of electricity

radiant energy   the energy created by the movement of atoms and molecules

Think about a car on a roller coaster. Write **P** where the greatest potential energy will be for the car. Write **K** where the greatest kinetic energy will be for the car.

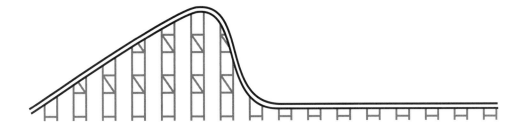

Write *true* or *false*.

1. _____ Radiant energy travels in circles.

2. _____ Some radiant energy comes from the sun.

3. _____ A microwave uses radiant energy to cook food.

4. _____ Each kind of radiant energy has a different wavelength.

5. _____ X-rays are the only kind of radiant energy that you can see.

6. _____ A television uses radiant energy in the form of radio waves.

How does energy change when you turn on a lamp?

_____

_____

How does energy change when you eat food?

_____

_____

Assessment

Assessment # 9

Answer the questions.

1. What are three different kinds of energy that are present in the class room? Name the kind of energy and describe its use.

    _____

    _____

    _____

2. How are radiant energy waves the same as and different from other kinds of waves?

    _____

    _____

    _____

3. Think about a skier on a snow-covered hill. How does the person change potential energy into kinetic energy?

    _____

    _____

    _____

Fill in the circle next to the best answer.

4. What kind of energy is an x-ray?

    (A) chemical   (C) mechanical

    (B) radiant   (D) electrical

5. How does a battery-operated watch change energy?

    (A) electrical to radiant   (C) chemical to mechanical

    (B) mechanical to electrical   (D) thermal to electrical

What kind of charge does this atom have? Explain.

_____

_____

What will happen to change the charge of this atom? Why?

_____

_____

Describe how charges between the ground and a cloud create lightning.

_____

_____

_____

_____

_____

Look at the diagram. Explain how an electric circuit works.

_____

_____

_____

_____

_____

Write numbers **1** through **5** to show how electricity is produced.

_____ The generator makes electricity.

_____ The turbine turns the drive shaft.

_____ Coal burns to power the turbine.

_____ Power lines deliver the electricity to the buildings.

_____ The drive shaft powers the electromagnet in the generator.

Assessment # 10

Fill in the circle next to the best answer.

1. What kind of charge does an atom with extra electrons have?

   (A) negative   (C) no charge

   (B) positive   (D) all of the above

2. Which unit measures how much electric energy a building uses?

   (A) kilowatt-hour   (C) watt

   (B) volt   (D) amps

3. Which material is not a conductor?

   (A) glass   (C) metal

   (B) plastic   (D) water

4. What is the power source for a generator in a power plant?

   (A) the sun   (C) electricity

   (B) electromagnets   (D) batteries

Answer the questions.

5. Why do some clothes stick together when they are pulled from a dryer?

   _____

   _____

   _____

6. How does the use of electricity affect your daily life? Give two examples in your explanation.

   _____

   _____

   _____

How are all sounds made?

_____

How do sounds travel? Explain the process.

_____

_____

_____

Draw a line to match each word to its definition.

wavelength   the highest point of a wave

crest   half the distance of a wavelength

trough   the lowest point of a wave

frequency   the number of waves that move past a point in a one second

amplitude   the distance from one point on a wave to the same point on the next wave

Write *true* or *false*.

1. _____ Pitch is the quality of being a high or low sound.

2. _____ Pitch is based on the amplitude of a sound wave.

3. _____ Sounds that have a high pitch have long wavelengths.

4. _____ A loud sound always has a high pitch.

5. _____ A sound having a low pitch has a low frequency.

What is the pitch and volume shown by the wavelength. Tell how you know.

_____

_____

_____

Draw a wavelength having the opposite pitch and volume.

Assessment

Assessment # 11

Look at the graph. Then, answer the questions.

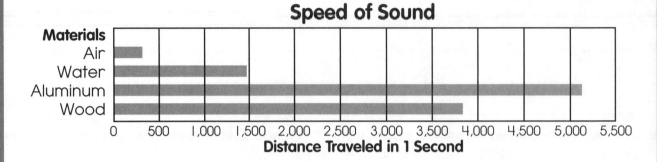

1. Of the materials on the graph, through which does sound travel the fastest?

_____

2. Why might sound travel more quickly through aluminum than air?

_____

_____

3. Why can't sound travel in space?

_____

_____

_____

Fill in the circle next to the best answer.

4. How does a guitar make a sound?

   (A) A string gets longer.   (C) The wood gets hot.

   (B) A string vibrates.   (D) The wood gets smaller.

5. Which instrument has the lowest pitch?

   (A) violin   (C) clarinet

   (B) cymbals   (D) bass drum

Write numbers **1** through **7** to show the order of the scientific classification system from general to specific. Then, write numbers **1** through **7** to show how human beings are classified.

_____ class		_____ Animal	
_____ genus		_____ Mammals	
_____ kingdom		_____ Vertebrate	
_____ species		_____ Carnivore	
_____ order		_____ Sapiens	
_____ phylum		_____ Primates	
_____ family		_____ Homo	

On the line in front of each kingdom, write one characteristic of those organisms. Then, draw a line to match each kingdom with an organism found in it.

_____	Moneran	eagle
_____	Protist	bacteria
_____	Fungus	mushroom
_____	Plant	daisy
_____	Animal	algae

Write **C** in front of each characteristic scientists use to classify organisms.

_____ cell structure		_____ how it gets energy
_____ height		_____ how it reproduces
_____ color		_____ how it smells
_____ body structure		_____ how it sees

Why do scientists want to classify animals?

_____

_____

Describe the two main groups of animals.

_____

_____

Describe three ways that scientist classify plants.

_____

_____

_____

Day #1

Day #2

Day #3

Day #4

Assessment

Assessment # 12

Answer the questions.

1. How is scientific classification a system?

_____

_____

_____

2. Can two different animals have the same scientific name? Why or why not?

_____

_____

_____

3. Describe three characteristics of moss that help scientist classify it.

_____

_____

4. Imagine that a new animal has been discovered. It has wings and flies. Its body is covered in fur, and it gives birth to live young, which it feeds milk. How would scientists classify this animal. What animal do you already know about that will help classify it? Explain.

_____

_____

_____

Fill in the circle next to the best answer.

5. Which of these is not a characteristic of a mammal?

(A) feeds its young milk   (C) has fur

(B) is cold-blooded   (D) has a vertebrate

What is a cell?

_____

List at least four of the six processes of life that cells control?

_____

_____

_____

Name the cell. Then, label its parts. Tell what each part does.

Name _____

_____

_____

_____

_____

_____

Name the cell. Then, label its parts. Tell what each part does.

Name _____

_____

_____

_____

_____

_____

_____

Write *true* or *false*.

1. _____ All cells have a nucleus.

2. _____ Chloroplasts are structures inside the cell's nucleus that control its activities.

3. _____ A cell will divide and make two cells that are the exact same.

4. _____ Organs are made of similar cells that work together.

5. _____ Chromosomes in one cell are the same as the other new cell.

Assessment

Assessment # 13

Answer the questions.

1. Identify three specific cells in the human body. Tell what process of life they control.

   _____

   _____

   _____

2. Is a virus a kind of cell? Why or why not?

   _____

   _____

3. How do cells help scientists classify animals into kingdoms?

   _____

   _____

   _____

4. Describe how cells divide.

   _____

   _____

   _____

   _____

Fill in the circle next to the best answer.

5. Which of the following is a single cell?

   (A) bacteria   (C) heart

   (B) moss   (D) blood

Name

Week #14: Heredity and Reproduction

Day #1

Write a word from the box to complete each definition.

| trait | inherit | heredity | reproduction | fertilization | species |

1. _____ – the passing of characteristics from one generation to the next
2. _____ – the process of making new organisms
3. _____ – a group of organisms that can reproduce
4. _____ – a feature or characteristic gotten from a parent
5. _____ – to get a characteristic from a parent or ancestor
6. _____ – the process when a sperm cell and egg cell join together

Day #2

What are three traits that organisms in the same species might have?

_____

_____

_____

What are three specific traits that you inherited from your parents?

_____

_____

Day #3

A plant produces both smooth and wrinkled seeds. The smooth seeds are dominant. The wrinkled seeds are recessive. Complete the Punnett square to show what the offspring of these two parent plants will be.

Predict what kinds of seed the offspring will have.

_____

_____

	S	S
S		
S		

Day #4

Unscramble the letters in bold to make words that tell about plant reproduction. Then, write numbers **1** through **6** to tell the order of plant reproduction.

_____ The bee takes the pollen to another plant and **lanstoplie** the pistil.

_____ Sperm cells, found in pollen, grow on the **matnes**. Egg cells are found in the ovules deep inside the **iplist**.

_____ A tube grows down from pollen through the pistil into an **lovue**.

_____ The fertilized egg **crudesrope**.

_____ The sperm cell **terzilfies** the egg cell.

_____ The **nelplo** sticks to the bee as it gathers nectar.

Assessment

Assessment # 14

Answer the questions.

1. How does heredity affect a species?

_____

_____

2. What are two ways that cells produce new organisms?

_____

_____

3. What are three factors affecting the growth and development of an organism?

_____

_____

_____

_____

4. Suppose one parent has brown eyes and another parent has blue eyes.

   Which color is dominant? _____

5. What combinations of genes might the parents describe above have? Use a capital **B** for dominant and lower case **b** for recessive. (Hint: There may be more than one.)

   brown eyes _____   blue eyes _____

6. Draw squares to show the gene combinations of eye color that the offspring might have.

What is an adaptation?

_____

_____

Choose an animal. What is one way its body is adapted to its environment?
What is one behavior that helps it adapt to its environment?

_____

_____

Write **B** if the adaptation is a behavior. Write **S** if the adaptation is related to structure.

_____ thick fur

_____ webbed feet

_____ flies away for winter

_____ builds a nest

_____ hisses at strangers

_____ leaves use sunlight for energy

Juan went to the zoo. He saw an animal with big ears, short brown fur that was peeking out of a whole in the ground. What are four inferences that Juan can make about the adaptations of the animal?

_____

_____

_____

_____

What is a mutation?

_____

How can a mutation positively and negatively affect a species?

_____

_____

_____

Assessment # 15

Answer the questions.

1. A brown bear and a squirrel belong to different species. Yet they have several adaptations that are the same. Identify one structural and one behavioral adaptation showing how they are alike. Then, explain how each adaptation helps them.

_____

_____

2. What is one inference that you can make based on the adaptations you cited in Question 1?

_____

_____

3. How do variations develop? What affect do they have on a species?

_____

_____

_____

4. Look at the illustration. What are two adaptations that help this organism live in its environment? Explain.

_____

_____

_____

_____

Unscramble the letters in bold to make a word that completes each sentence.

1. All living things need **greeny** to survive.
2. Plants are **crodupres** that use light to make energy.
3. Animals are **smonsruce** because they eat plants and other animals.
4. An **evibrroeh** is an animal that eats plants to get the stored energy of sugar.
5. A **anorvecri** is an animal that eats other animals to get the stored energy of nutrients.
6. An **ermovnio** is an animal that gets energy from both plants and animals.

Day #1

What are two ways that the energy stored in dead organisms is used? Give examples of each.

_____

_____

What is the relationship between decomposers and plants?

_____

_____

Day #2

Look at the illustration. Draw a picture of four other animals to show how energy moves in a food chain.

Use the unscrambled words from Day 1 to label the organisms in your chain.

Day #3

Compare a food chain and a food web. Tell how they are alike and different.

_____

_____

_____

Look at the chain you made in Day 3. What organisms can you include to show a food web? Write at least three more animals' names and draw arrows to show a food web.

What ecosystem does your web represent? _____

Day #4

Assessment

Assessment # 16

Fill in the circle next to the best answer?

1. What is the main source of energy for plants?

    (A) sugar   (C) decomposers

    (B) nutrients   (D) oxygen

2. What does the diagram below show?

    (A) an ecosystem   (C) an energy pyramid

    (B) a food chain   (D) a food web

Answer the questions.

3. Explain the flow of energy in the diagram. Use the words in the box to help you.

| photosynthesis | producer | consumer | energy | predator | prey |

_____

_____

_____

_____

_____

Draw a line to match each word to its meaning.

ecosystem   the place an animal lives where all its needs can be met

habitat   all the populations that live in a place

population   all the living and nonliving things in a place

environment   a group of one kind of living thing that lives in a place

community   everything that is around a living thing

Why do scientists keep track of populations? Explain.

_____

_____

Animals often move around. How might scientist keep track of the animals in these populations?

_____

_____

What are three reasons that a population might change?

_____

_____

How might an increasing population of robins positively and negatively affect a community?

_____

_____

The Siberian tiger is on the endangered list. What does this mean?

_____

Why is it important that an animal not become extinct?

_____

_____

_____

Assessment # 17

Look at the graph. Then, answer the questions.

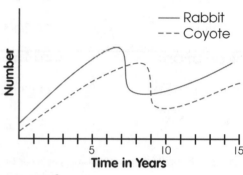

1. What happened to the rabbit population for the first six years?

   _____

   _____

2. When did the coyote population begin to increase?

   _____

   _____

3. What reason might have contributed to the increase in the coyote population?

   _____

   _____

   _____

4. Why is the line graph a good choice to communicate data?

   _____

   _____

5. How does the graph help you understand the balance of nature?

   _____

   _____

   _____

   _____

Name

Label the four layers of Earth. Write one fact about each layer.

_____

_____

_____

_____

_____

_____

Compare the three parts of the mantle.

_____

_____

How does the outer core compare to the inner core? Tell how they are alike and different.

_____

_____

Write *true* or *false*.

1. _____ The thickest part of the crust is about 25 miles thick.
2. _____ Scientists believe that the continents were joined long ago.
3. _____ The surface of Earth is made up of seven plates.
4. _____ Each plate has either a continental crust or ocean crust on it.
5. _____ Plate tectonics explains how the continents move.
6. _____ The plates slowly move sideways when the heated molten rock in the core rises and cools.

Unscramble the letters in bold to make words that tell about plate movement. Then, write numbers **1** through **5** to tell the order of movement.

_____ As the molten rock gets near the crust, it cools and flows **wedisays**, pushed aside as more molten rock rises.

_____ The sideways movement of the mantle makes the **slepta** move sideways, too.

_____ The rocks **lemt** as they rise.

_____ The cooled rock in the mantle **kniss** back to the bottom.

_____ Heat in the bottom of the **tenlam** makes the solid rock flow.

Assessment

Assessment # 18

Answer the questions.

1. Is plate tectonics a cycle? Why or why not?

_____

_____

2. What are two formations resulting from plate movement? Describe how each happens.

_____

_____

_____

_____

3. Which two pieces of evidence helped scientists understand plate movement?

_____

_____

_____

Fill in the circle next to the best answer.

4. In what stage of the scientific process is plate tectonics?

(A) hypothesis   (C) theory

(B) experiment   (D) law

5. What force causes the denser ocean plates to sink under a continental plate when they collide?

(A) friction   (C) thermal

(B) magnetism   (D) gravity

Name _____

What is a natural resource?

_____

_____

List two living and two nonliving natural resources. Tell how each is a resource.

_____

_____

_____

_____

Day #1

Use each word in a sentence to show its meaning. Then, give an example of each.

renewable resource _____

_____

nonrenewable resource _____

_____

inexhaustible resource _____

_____

Day #2

How is soil a resource? What kind of resource is it?

_____

_____

The graph shows the materials in soil. How does knowing this help a farmer protect this important resource?

_____

_____

minerals 45%

humus 5%

air 25%

water 25%

Day #3

List six ways people use water.

_____

_____

_____

What are three ways that people can conserve water?

_____

_____

Day #4

Assessment # 19

Fill in the circle next to the best answer.

1. Which is a fossil fuel?

   Ⓐ petroleum

   Ⓑ aluminum

   Ⓒ iron

   Ⓓ oxygen

2. Which is an inexhaustible resource?

   Ⓐ trees

   Ⓑ wind

   Ⓒ soil

   Ⓓ natural gas

Answer the questions.

3. Can a renewable resource ever be an inexhaustible resource? Explain.

   _____

   _____

   _____

   _____

4. Scientists estimate that the world's supply of petroleum is running out quickly. How will this impact you? How will this impact society? Should people promote stronger conservation measures to slow the loss of this resource? Write a paragraph discussing your opinions.

   _____

   _____

   _____

   _____

   _____

   _____

Tell how each event changes the surface of Earth.

volcano _____

_____

earthquake _____

_____

flood _____

_____

Write **C** if the statement describes chemical weathering. Write **P** if the statement describe physical weathering.

1. _____ A cave forms under the ground in limestone rock.
2. _____ Plant roots grow in the crack of a rock and force the rock to crack.
3. _____ Air pollution wears away the nose on a statue.
4. _____ Water trickles in the crack of a rock and freezes, making the crack bigger.
5. _____ Wind picks up particles of sand and blasts the rock, forming an arch.
6. _____ The acid in a moss begins to wear a hole in a rock.

What is the difference in weathering and erosion?

_____

_____

What are the three forces that cause erosion?

_____

How does a glacier cause erosion?

_____

Circle the word that best completes each sentence.

1. (Weathering, Deposition) is the settling of rocks and soil once it has been eroded.
2. The materials fall out once the water or wind (quickens, slows).
3. The soil in these areas is filled with rich (nutrients, gases) that are good for crops.
4. Depositions caused by wind can form (mountains, dunes).
5. Depositions caused by ocean water can form new (bays, beaches).
6. In a river, deposition can create a (delta, canyon).

Assessment # 20

Answer the questions.

1. What are four ways that rocks are physically weathered to form soil. Explain each way.

_____

_____

_____

_____

_____

2. Can a river change the land? Explain.

_____

_____

_____

3. How can a piece of a rock from a mountain end up in a river delta? Use the words in the box in your explanation.

| deposition | erosion | weathering |

_____

_____

_____

_____

Fill in the circle next to the best answer.

4. Which helps prevent soil erosion?

(A) spraying water   (C) planting grass

(B) plowing fields   (D) constructing buildings

Write words from the box to complete each statement.

stratosphere troposphere mesosphere atmosphere exosphere thermosphere gravity

1. The _____ is about 500 miles high.
2. It is held close to Earth because of _____.
3. We live in the _____.
4. The top layer, which is space, is the _____.
5. Ozone gas is in the _____ layer.
6. Space shuttles travel in the _____.
7. Meteors burn up in the _____.

Day #1

Label the diagram. Use the words from Day 1 to help you.

Day #2

What are the three most important gases in the troposphere? Tell why each is important.

_____

_____

_____

_____

_____

Day #3

Write *true* or *false*.

1. _____ Most of the air in the troposphere is made of oxygen.
2. _____ Lightning can make nitrogen gas in the air useable to organisms.
3. _____ Some bacteria can also make nitrogen gas useable to organisms.
4. _____ Plants do not need nitrogen.
5. _____ Decomposers change oxygen in dead organisms into nitrogen gas.
6. _____ The nitrogen levels are constantly decreasing each year.

Day #4

Assessment

Assessment # 21

Answer the questions.

1. A farmer rotates planting clover and corn in a field each year. Why does he do this? What role does the atmosphere have in the process?

___

___

___

2. In what layer will you find ozone gas? Why is this gas important?

___

___

___

3. Look at the chart. It tells the amounts of each kind of gas in the troposphere. Make a circle graph to show the data.

Gas	Percentages (%)
Nitrogen	78
Oxygen	21
Carbon dioxide	0.9
Other	0.1

4. Why is a circle graph a good way to show the data?

___

___

Fill in the circle next to the best answer.

5. Jason saw a shooting star. In which layer of the atmosphere was it?

   (A) troposphere
   (B) stratosphere
   (C) mesosphere
   (D) exosphere

What is the temperature shown on the thermometer? _____

°C   30   20   10   0   10   20   30   40

About what temperature would it be on the Fahrenheit scale? _____

What activity would you most likely do in this kind of weather?

_____

What is weather?

_____

How does climate differ from weather?

_____

_____

What is the climate in the community in which you live?

_____

How does the shape of Earth affect climate?

_____

_____

_____

How does the tilt of Earth affect climate?

_____

_____

Label the diagram. Use the words in the box.

| dry air |
| moist air |
| snow |
| rain |
| ocean |
| mountain |

Assessment

Assessment # 22

Answer the questions.

1. What is one natural event and one human activity that can affect climate? How does this impact the balance of nature?

_____

_____

_____

_____

2. The chart below shows the average monthly temperatures and rainfall in Austin, Texas. Use the data to make a line graph of the temperatures.

Month	Temperature (°F)	Precipitation (in.)
Jan.	60	1.9
Feb.	65	2.0
Mar.	73	2.1
Apr.	79	2.5
May	85	5.0
June	91	3.8
July	95	2.0
Aug.	96	2.3
Sept.	90	2.9
Oct.	81	4.0
Nov.	70	2.7
Dec.	62	2.4

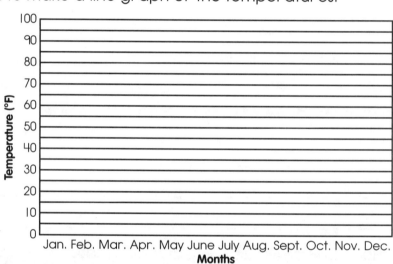

3. What is the climate of this place? Explain how you know.

_____

_____

_____

4. How does climate affect people? Name two ways.

_____

_____

Draw a line to match each word with its definition.

planet   a rocky object that revolves around the sun

star   a group of stars that forms a pattern in the night sky

asteroid   a ball of burning gases

meteorite   a large group of stars surrounded by gas and dust

comet   a large space object that revolves around the sun

constellation   a ball of ice, gas, and dust that moves orbits around the sun

galaxy   a rocky object from space that travel through the atmosphere and lands on the surface of Earth

Day #1

Write *true* or *false*.

1. _____ Scientists measure a star's distance from Earth in meters.
2. _____ Planets move in an elliptical path.
3. _____ Gravity is the force that keeps the planets orbiting around the sun.
4. _____ The asteroid belt is located between Jupiter and Saturn.
5. _____ A shooting star is actually a meteoroid that enters Earth's atmosphere.
6. _____ Planets shine because they reflect the light from a star.

Day #2

How do atoms make stars burn?

_____
_____
_____

What are three properties that scientists use to classify stars?

_____
_____

Day #3

Akio and his sister, Mori, are looking at the night sky. Akio points out one star that is particularly bright. His sister says it is not a star. Why might Mori make this statement? Explain.

_____

What hypothesis might Akio make?

_____

How could he prove the hypothesis?

_____

Day #4

Assessment

Assessment # 23

Answer the questions.

1. How is a comet the same as and different from Earth?

   _____

   _____

2. Suppose you see two stars of equal brightness. Are they the same distance from Earth? Explain.

   _____

   _____

3. What are three characteristics that allow Earth to support life? Explain why each is important.

   _____

   _____

   _____

4. Explain what is happening in the diagram.

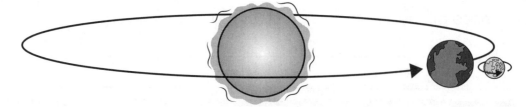

   _____

   _____

Fill in the circle next to the best answer.

5. What makes a meteorite burn?

   (A) gas   (C) magnetism

   (B) friction   (D) potential energy

What is the hardware of the computer?

_____

_____

Name three pieces of hardware and their functions.

_____

_____

_____

Day #1

What does the software of the computer do?

_____

_____

Name three kinds of software and their uses.

_____

_____

_____

Day #2

Mia made a document on her computer to show the money she earned. What kind of document is this?

_____

Explain how Mia will find out how much she earned walking dogs.

_____

_____

	A	B	C	D
1	**Money Earned**			
2	Date	Baby-sitting	Dog Walking	Total
3	June 12		$5.00	$5.00
4	June 13	$15.00	$5.00	$20.00
5	June 14	$12.00	$5.00	$17.00
6	June 15		$10.00	$10.00
7	June 16	$18.00		
8	Total			

Day #3

What are three reasons you use the Internet?

_____

_____

What are two benefits of e-mail?

_____

_____

Day #4

Assessment

Assessment # 24

Answer the questions.

1. Label the tool bar to show what each function does.

2. What are three safety rules that you should follow while using the Internet? Why are these rules important?

_____

_____

_____

3. What are two positive and two negative aspects of computers in our society?

_____

_____

_____

4. Think about all the places that use computers, including school, stores, transportation, and home. How do computers impact your daily life?

_____

_____

_____

_____

The National Aeronautics and Space Administration, or NASA, is the agency in the United States government that works to understand outer space. They send spacecraft and astronauts up to explore this last frontier.

What are three specific problems that people in space must deal with?

_____

_____

How are these problems solved?

_____

NASA scientists look at specific problems and find ways to solve them. They develop materials and tools that keep the vehicles and people safe. Many of these materials are now a part of our daily lives. For example, astronauts needed to drill holes into the moon to get rock samples. The tool needed to have its own power source. A tool company invented cordless tools to solve the problem.

Why would a drill need to have its own power source in space?

_____

_____

If you look up at the ceiling outside the bedrooms or kitchen, you will most likely see a smoke detector. Smoke detectors were first used on the Skylab Space Station in the 1970s. The space station was the first environment for astronauts to live in away from Earth.

Why is the smoke detector useful in our daily lives?

_____

_____

_____

Food that is freeze-dried has no moisture. As a result, it is very lightweight, stores compactly, and does not need refrigeration. Moreover, freeze-dried food can last for years. It was another NASA invention. Today, these packets of food are popular with hikers and campers.

Why was freeze-dried food important for space travel?

_____

_____

_____

Assessment

Assessment # 25

Read the paragraph. Then, answer the questions.

Racecar drivers use two inventions that were first developed for astronauts. The suits they wear have a special coating that is less likely to burn. However, these suits can also trap the body's heat, making the suit very hot to wear. So racecar drivers also use another NASA technology, called *cool suits*. A special garment is worn next to the body under the suit. Chilled liquid is pumped throughout the garment.

1. What problems did each kind of clothing solve for astronauts?

    _____

    _____

2. Why would the suits with a special coating that did not burn be good for a racecar driver?

    _____

    _____

3. How do you think a cool suit rids the body of heat?

    _____

    _____

4. How else might a cool suit be used?

    _____

    _____

5. How does communication between scientists affect society?

    _____

    _____

Asthma is a disease where the airways in the lungs get blocked. Breathing may be difficult at times for people experiencing this illness. People with asthma may blow into a peak flow meter daily. This simple device measures how much air is being expelled. If the level is low, the person knows that an attack is about to happen and can take medicine to prevent it.

Why would a person with asthma want to know if an attack is about to happen?

_____

_____

You feel hot and have a headache. You wonder if you have a fever. You walk to the medicine cabinet to get out a thermometer. Then, you stick it in your ear. This kind of thermometer measures the heat, in the form of infrared radiation, coming from your eardrum. It's quick and very accurate, too.

Compare an ear thermometer with the one you use. How is the ear thermometer better? How is it worse?

_____

_____

Long ago, doctors used cotton thread to sew the skin together to close a deep cut. The patient would have to return later to have them taken out. Today, doctors have different ways to close the skin. People can get stitches that dissolve. The doctor uses thread made of natural materials, like silk and hair, that the body's chemicals break down easily.

Why are stitches that dissolve an improvement over those of cotton thread?

_____

_____

Another way to close a wound is with skin glue. This method is often chosen if the wound is straight and not too deep. A trained professional holds the edges of the skin closed while applying a layer of special glue. The glue dries quickly. It can bend and keep moisture out of the wound. By the time the wound heals, the glue has worn off.

Who might benefit the most from using skin glue? Why?

_____

_____

Assessment

Assessment # 26

Read the paragraph. Then, answer the questions.

Jon Comer is a professional skateboarder who attends competitions around the world. He drops into a half-pipe and does many amazing tricks. What is really amazing is that Comer has an artificial limb, called a *prosthetic*, on one leg. Scientists join technology and science to help many people like Comer. The limbs are made of a kind of flexible plastics with a microprocessor inside. When joined to the body, muscle movement is changed to electric signals, which makes the artificial limb move.

1. What do you think the microprocessor does in prosthetics?

    _____

    _____

    _____

    _____

2. Why is it important that science and technology work together? Give three reasons.

    _____

    _____

    _____

    _____

    _____

    _____

    _____

    _____

Name _____

What is a telescope? How does it work?

_____

_____

How is an optical telescope different from a radio telescope?

_____

_____

_____

Label the lens. Draw lines to show how light moves through it. Then, describe the movement.

_____

_____

_____

_____

_____

Label the lens. Draw lines to show how light moves through it. Then, describe the movement.

_____

_____

_____

_____

_____

The Hubble Space Telescope orbits above Earth's atmosphere. It is a reflecting telescope that is about the size of a school bus. It senses infrared, ultraviolet, and visible light, taking pictures of the images and sending the information to scientists on Earth.

Why would scientists want to put a telescope in space?

_____

_____

_____

Assessment

Assessment # 27

Read the paragraph. Then, answer the questions.

Galileo did not build the first refracting telescope, but he improved it. Experimenting with convex lens, he was the first person to clearly view craters on Earth's moon. Another great scientist, Sir Isaac Newton, experimented with light. He found that using a concave mirror, flat mirror, and a convex lens made the heavenly views clearer and closer. His telescope became known as the reflecting telescope.

1. Think about the names of the two telescopes. How does each use light?

_____

_____

2. Choose one scientist mentioned in the paragraph. Give two reasons why he was a good scientist.

_____

_____

_____

3. Why do scientists want to study space?

_____

_____

_____

Fill in the circle next to the best answer.

4. Why does a radio telescope have a reflector that is shaped like a dish?

(A) It spreads out the waves so the antenna can read them.

(B) It catches the waves and focuses them on the antenna.

(C) It focuses the waves to a point on the lens.

(D) It spreads out the waves so the lens can collect the light.

How are natural and human-made satellites the same and different?

_____

_____

_____

List two examples of each.

_____

_____

What is the purpose of a scientific satellite?

_____

_____

_____

How would this satellite help scientists?

_____

_____

List three conditions a weather satellite tracks.

_____

_____

_____

How does the information from a weather satellite help people on Earth?

_____

_____

What kind of satellite does a cell phone need?

_____

_____

What would your life be like without this satellite?

_____

_____

Name

Assessment # 28

Answer the questions.

1. Some governments launch military satellites to track the movements of people, vehicles, and missiles in other countries. Do you think this is a good idea? Write a paragraph that explains your opinion and if it is a morally responsible practice.

_____

_____

_____

_____

_____

_____

2. What happens to a satellite that stops working or is no longer needed?

_____

_____

_____

3. Think about the many different satellites and their uses. Which do you think impacts your life the most? Why?

_____

_____

_____

Fill in the circle next to the best answer.

4. Which kind of satellite would a global positioning system (GPS) use?

(A) navigation   (C) communication

(B) military   (D) scientific

Write the name of the system described in each statement.

1. The bones support the body, give it shape, and protect the soft parts. _____

2. The body uses energy when food is broken down. _____
3. Muscles help the body move. _____
4. Waste is removed from the body. _____
5. Oxygen enters the body, and carbon dioxide leaves the body. _____
6. The brain and nerves control the whole body. _____
7. Red blood cells deliver oxygen to all parts of your body. _____

Write numbers **1** through **6** to show the order of the respiratory system.

_____ Air flows through the trachea.

_____ Oxygen passes into red bloods cells in blood vessels.

_____ Air enters the nose.

_____ Inside the lungs, air passes through smaller tubes to reach the alveoli.

_____ Carbon dioxide enters the air sacs and leaves the body.

_____ Air flows through the bronchial tubes into the lungs.

Write *true* or *false* to tell about the circulatory system.

1. _____ The heart, brain, blood, and blood vessels make up the circulatory system.
2. _____ Nutrients travel by blood to the cells in the body.
3. _____ White blood cells inside the blood help fight infections.
4. _____ The smallest blood vessels are called *veins*.
5. _____ The circulatory system controls body temperature.
6. _____ The circulatory system moves oxygen throughout your body.

Unscramble the letters in bold to make a word that completes each sentence about the nervous system.

1. The **sovernu** system helps people sense their environment.
2. It consists of the **nabir**, spinal cord, and nerves.
3. Outside **preetrocs**, like the eyes, ears, and skin, recognize changes.
4. Inside **sronag**, like the heart and stomach, sense changes in chemicals and body fluids.
5. The information travels through the nerves and **niplas** cord to the brain.
6. The brain processes the information and sends a signal telling the body how to **crate**.

Day #1 Day #2 Day #3 Day #4

Assessment # 29

Answer the questions.

1. Are all parts in a human body system important? Explain.

_____

_____

_____

_____

2. Ed is studying the digestive system in school. He learns that digestion begins in the mouth. What experiment can Ed do prove it? Plan an experiment. Include the problem, hypothesis, and experimentation steps.

_____

_____

_____

_____

_____

_____

_____

Fill in the circle next to the best answer.

3. What do cells need to release energy in the body?

   (A) oxygen and proteins   (C) nitrogen and carbon dioxide

   (B) sugar and carbon dioxide   (D) oxygen and sugar

4. Why does the body excrete water?

   (A) to maintain a steady body temperature   (C) to raise the body temperature

   (B) to lower the body temperature   (D) to record the body temperature

Why is it important to eat a healthy diet? Give two reasons.

_____

_____

_____

Why should you eat foods of all different colors?

_____

_____

Name three ways that exercise helps the body.

_____

_____

_____

Do you get enough exercise? Why or why not?

_____

_____

What is hygiene?

_____

_____

What are three good hygiene practices you follow?

_____

_____

_____

Draw a line to match each word with its definition.

drugs	a mental or physical need to use a drug
prescription drugs	chemicals that a person can buy in a store
illegal drugs	using drugs for reasons other than health
dependence	a chemical in cigarettes that makes the heart beat faster
nicotine	chemicals that are not allowed by law
alcohol	chemicals that change the way the body works
drug abuse	a liquid chemical that slows the brain

Assessment # 30

1. Why is it important to warm up and cool down before exercising?

_____

_____

2. Why are safety rules important? Include three examples of rules you follow in your explanation.

_____

_____

_____

_____

3. A friend begins smoking a cigarette. What will you say and do?

_____

_____

_____

_____

Fill in the circle next to the best answer.

4. Which is not a nutrient your body needs?

   (A) proteins   (C) sugars

   (B) carbohydrates   (D) fats

5. To which drug can people form a dependence?

   (A) alcohol   (C) marijuana

   (B) nicotine   (D) all of the above

Write a word from the box to correctly complete each sentence. Use each word one time.

| virus | fungi | bacteria | pathogens | communicable |

1. A _____ disease is an illness that spreads from person to person.
2. These diseases are spread through _____, such as bacteria and viruses.
3. Some _____ are harmful and produce toxins that cause illnesses, like strep throat.
4. A _____ enters a cell and reproduces rapidly, taking over its function.
5. Some _____ cause skin infections, like athlete's foot.

Describe four ways that communicable diseases are spread.

_____
_____
_____
_____
_____

Look at the four actions you listed above. Tell a way to prevent each.

_____
_____
_____
_____
_____

Write *true* or *false*.

1. _____ A noncommunicable disease can be spread by sneezing.
2. _____ Heredity and a person's environment can cause a noncommunicable disease.
3. _____ Some people have allergies and react to specific materials with which they come into contact.
4. _____ Plants cannot cause allergies.
5. _____ People with allergies may get a skin rash or frequently sneeze.
6. _____ Cancer is a disease that can spread between people.

Assessment

Assessment # 31

Answer the questions.

1. How are bacteria and viruses the same and different?

_____

_____

2. Can the body develop an immunity to disease? Explain.

_____

_____

_____

_____

3. How does your body help fight disease? Identify three ways.

_____

_____

_____

_____

4. What is a vaccine? How does a vaccine prevent a disease?

_____

_____

Fill in the circle next to the best answer.

5. Which is a noncommunicable disease?

(A) malaria   (C) small pox

(B) hemophilia   (D) rabies

Name

Write a word to correctly complete each sentence.
1. Adding harmful materials to the environment causes _____.
2. Dumping trash on the ground results in _____ pollution.
3. Construction sights using heavy equipment and loud music produce _____ pollution.
4. Sewage and oil leaks into ponds, lakes, streams, and oceans make _____ pollution.
5. _____ pollution is a huge problem because it affects our breathing and temperature balance on Earth.
6. People are also concerned about _____ pollution in big cities because bright lights make it difficult to see the stars at night.

Write *true* or *false*.

1. _____ Most of the world's fresh water is contained in glaciers.
2. _____ There is more fresh water than salt water.
3. _____ Some people get their water from lakes.
4. _____ Groundwater can become polluted by runoff of water from farms.
5. _____ Farmers put fertilizer in their wastewater to make it safe to use.
6. _____ Washing your hands and brushing your teeth adds to water pollution.

Tyler heard on the news that the city he lives in has lots of air pollution. He does an experiment where he spreads petroleum jelly on paper. He puts the paper outside in the morning, and then checks it before dinner. The jelly has lots of dirt and dust on it.

What might have been Tyler's hypothesis?

_____

Did Tyler's experiment prove his hypothesis? Explain.

_____

What are three ways that the land gets polluted?

_____

_____

_____

List two ways that land pollution can affect you?

_____

_____

Assessment

Assessment # 32

Answer the questions.

1. Can the music you listen to cause noise pollution? Explain.

   _____

   _____

   _____

2. Which form of pollution is the biggest problem in your community? Identify it, its causes, and its effects. Then, suggest a way tell how to solve the problem.

   _____

   _____

   _____

   _____

   _____

   _____

   _____

Fill in the circle next to the best answer.

3. Which is not a pollutant?

   (A) a jack hammer   (C) fertilizer

   (B) volcanic ash   (D) water

4. What is the main contribution to rising ozone levels?

   (A) burning fossil fuels   (C) sunlight

   (B) space debris   (D) tree cutting

What are three ways that people change the land?

_____

_____

_____

How do people benefit from each change you listed?

_____

_____

Look at the changes you listed in Day 1. What is one way that each change negatively affects people?

_____

_____

Do the benefits outweigh the negative affects in your examples? Explain.

_____

_____

Ozone is a gas found in the stratosphere. How does it help people?

_____

What are people doing that affect the ozone?

_____

What are two effects that will most likely occur if the ozone continues to be destroyed?

_____

_____

As the human population grew in the United States, people built houses on farmland. This growth caused a decrease in the bluebird population. These birds nested in tree holes they found near open fields. People in some communities began to build special boxes for the birds, placing them in parks and backyards. The bluebird population began to grow again.

What were two negative and positive impacts of human beings on the bluebird population?

_____

Assessment

Assessment # 33

Read the paragraph. Then, answer the questions.

Kudzu is a plant indigenous to Japan. It grows quickly and has beautiful, fragrant flowers. People brought it to the United States to help prevent soil erosion, feed animals, and decorate gardens. However, kudzu grew so well in the south, that it totally covered many native flowers, shrubs, and trees, killing the plants. The United States Department of Agriculture declared that kudzu was a weed in 1972 and began killing it. The plant, needing several applications of herbicides, was hard to kill. In the meantime, several people worked to find uses for the plant. They make baskets, jelly, and syrup from kudzu. Preliminary testing also shows that it may one day be made into a useful drug.

1. How did the decision to plant kudzu negatively impact the U.S.?

    _____

    _____

2. How did the decision positively impact the U.S.?

    _____

    _____

3. Why did people change their view of kudzu?

    _____

    _____

4. Is kudzu a resource? Explain.

    _____

    _____

5. Why did the native plants die?

    _____

Which kind of trash is thrown out the most?

Trash Thrown Out in the United States

_____

What are three specific kinds of this trash that you throw out at school or home?

_____

_____

_____

Paper 40%
Yard Trimmings 18%
Metals 8%
Plastics 8%
Glass 7%
Other 12%
(rubber, leather, cloth, wood, misc.)
Food Scraps 7%

What are the three R's for helping the environment? Write a sentence using each word and tell how you practice each.

_____

_____

_____

_____

_____

Write numbers **1** through **5** to show the order of the steps to recycle aluminum cans.

_____ The melted aluminum is pored into bar molds and cooled.

_____ The old cans are melted in a furnace.

_____ The old cans are crushed and shredded.

_____ The aluminum bars are shaped into cans, foil, automobile parts, or doors.

_____ Old aluminum cans are collected.

Recycling an aluminum can takes less energy than making a new one from bauxite. Why?

_____

_____

How does buying a product in bulk help the environment?

_____

_____

Assessment

Assessment # 34

Answer the questions.

1. How does reducing solid waste help Earth? Explain three ways.

_____

_____

_____

2. What might happen to Earth if people do not reduce solid wastes? List three effects.

_____

_____

_____

3. Yard clippings, orange peels, coffee grounds, and other food scraps can be put into a mulch pile. Explain what a mulch pile is, how it works, and what it can be used for. Use the words in the box in your explanation.

energy	nutrients	decomposers	decay

_____

_____

_____

_____

_____

Fill in the circle next to the best answer.

4. Which product is made from recycled rubber?

(A) running tracks   (C) coffee mugs

(B) playground slides   (D) windows

The ancient Egyptians spent much time looking up at the sky and made two basic discoveries that affect our daily life. First, they gave us the measurement of time in the form of a 24-hour day. They also fixed the year to include 365 days.

What two cycles did the Egyptians use to help them measure time? Explain.

_____

_____

_____

Hygiene was important to the Egyptians. Water was in great supply, so they washed often. They reduced odors by placing small balls of incense and porridge where body limbs met. The people chewed herbs and used milk as a gargle to make the breath smell better. Wealthy women used cleansing cream made of oil and lime.

What products do you use today that are like the ones used by Egyptians?

_____

_____

The ancient Egyptians are also one of the earliest civilizations to use make-up. They lined their eyes with green malachite or black kohl. They ground colored minerals and mixed them with water to make a paste to apply to the eyelid. They combined fat and other red minerals to make lip color. Finally, red ochre and fat was combined to make a cheek color. They applied the make-up with sticks.

How are the Egyptian make-up products the same as and different from the ones people use today?

_____

_____

Information written on papyrus tell how early Egyptian doctors used the plants around them as medicines. They used onions to prevent colds and thyme as a pain reliever. Aloe vera was used to treat headaches, burns, and skin diseases. They used honey for a number of illnesses, from sore throats to antibiotics to spread on wounds.

Why were the early doctors good scientists?

_____

_____

Assessment

Assessment # 35

Read the paragraph. Then, answer the questions.

The Egyptians are best known for the pyramids. They used astronomy, engineering, and architecture to build these mammoth buildings. The four sides of each pyramid line up exactly north, south, east, and west. The Egyptians used the stars to achieve the perfect alignment. The huge limestone blocks were cut from nearby quarries. To move the massive stones, scientists believe the Egyptians floated them on barges down the river. Then they may have watered the sand or spread slick Nile River mud along the path to help them drag the stones on wooden sleds to the building site. Once at the site, they used ramps and poles to push the blocks into place.

1. How did the Egyptians use astronomy to build the pyramids?

_____

_____

2. What force did the Egyptians overcome to move the blocks across the sand? Explain.

_____

_____

3. How did the Egyptians use three resources to build the pyramids?

_____

_____

_____

4. How do we know about the contributions of the Egyptians? List two ways.

_____

_____

In the late 1700s, people began using steam as a source of energy in manufacturing. Nicolas-Joseph Cugnot thought that it would be a possible to use the steam engine for transportation. From 1769 to 1770, he built two self-propelled, steam-powered vehicles. One carried passengers, and the other was a tractor to move war supplies. The vehicles blew huge clouds of steam into the air, and they required a lot of work to keep the steam pressure up.

How did the steam engine create energy?

_____

_____

The modern car did not develop until the invention of the internal combustion engine. In 1860, Jean Lenoir invented an engine where coal gas exploded to make an energy source. In 1863, using petroleum as the fuel, he built the engine in a wagon and drove it 50 miles.

Even though Lenoir had an engine that worked, why do you think that he kept trying to improve it?

_____

_____

The first electric car was built in 1891. It ran on batteries and could carry six passengers. The cars became very popular because they were quiet, lacked the smoke and fumes of the steam-powered cars, and were easily operated. However, the batteries allowed the car to only go about 50 miles before being recharged, and they did not go very fast.

Compare the steam-powered and electric cars. How were they alike? How were they different?

_____

_____

As cars became more efficient and easier to drive, the demand for them increased. The assembly line made it possible to mass-produce cars quickly and cheaply. In 1913, Henry Ford built a manufacturing factory that had a conveyor belt. Workers were able to build a car in 93 minutes.

What two problems did Ford solve with his conveyor built?

_____

_____

_____

Assessment # 36

1. Use the information from the week to complete a timeline to show the history of the automobile.

1750   1775   1800   1825   1850   1875   1900   1925

2. How might a scientist use a timeline?

_____

_____

3. How can an invention lead to other technological developments that improve society? Give two examples based on the history of automobile.

_____

_____

4. How are the cars of today the same as and different from the early cars? Give two examples of each.

_____

_____

5. Think about the impact of the automobile on society. Most cars run on petroleum-based fuel. Since it is nonrenewable resource and quickly running out, what do you think happen to cars?

_____

_____

Isaac Newton is one of the most famous scientists in history. His first experiments dealt with bending light using a prism. After much experimentation, Newton discovered that white light could be separated into colors as it moved through a prism. Newton stated that light consisted of streams of very small particles. He shared his ideas in a journal, but they were not accepted because other scientists were unable to duplicate his experiments.

How might failures and not being accepted by peers encourage a scientist?

_____

_____

Day #1

Newton was interested in many other relationships in the universe. He used mathematics to study the idea that a force kept objects in motion. This idea led him to propose that gravity helped the large bodies, like Earth, orbit around the sun. Several people challenged Newton, which made him suggest that unseen particles were the reason for gravity.

Why did Newton continue to believe in his gravity theory when other doubted him?

_____

_____

Day #2

Newton began to look at how different things move, including sound. He calculated the speed of sound through air.

Why are Newton's calculations important today?

_____

_____

_____

_____

Day #3

Newton is best known for his three laws of motion. The first law states that all objects stay in rest or in a straight line of motion unless acted on by another force. The second law states that when a force is applied to an object, it will change its speed or direction. This law also states that more force is needed to move or stop something with a larger mass than something with a smaller mass. Finally, the third law states that when a force is applied to something, it will push back with an equal force.

Why are Newton's ideas about motion scientific laws?

_____

Day #4

Assessment # 37

Answer the questions.

1. Was Newton a good scientist? Why or why not? Support your opinions with three examples.

_____

_____

_____

_____

_____

_____

2. Give an example of each law of motion.

Law 1: _____

_____

Law 2: _____

_____

Law3: _____

_____

Fill in the circle next to the best answer.

3. What kind of experiments did Newton do with the prism?

  (A) reflecting light   (C) reflecting sound

  (B) refracting light   (D) refracting sound

4. What force is shown in Newton's first law of motion?

  (A) sound   (C) inertia

  (B) gravity   (D) light

Write a word to complete each sentence telling about fossils.

1. A _____ is the hollow remains shaped like an organism.
2. A _____ is an animal that lived long ago, but is now extinct.
3. Some organisms got trapped in the resin of a tree that has hardened, becoming _____.
4. People who study fossils are _____.
5. A _____ is the shape of an organism that is filled with sediment.
6. Sediment can replace particles of an ancient organism, becoming _____.

Write numbers **1** through **5** to show how a fossil is made.

_____ The soft parts rot.

_____ Layers of small rocks, sand, and mud cover the organism.

_____ The plant or animal dies.

_____ A print of the organism remains in the rock.

_____ The pressure of the layers of sediment forms rock.

Identify two reasons that scientists study fossils.

_____

_____

How can knowing about organisms living today help scientists understand about life long ago?

_____

_____

What kind of rock is shown here?

_____

Explain how you know.

_____

_____

_____

Assessment # 38

Assessment

Answer the questions.

1. How can studying fossils help scientists learn about Earth's history? Give three examples.

_____

_____

_____

_____

_____

2. Order the time periods from oldest to the most recent.

_____ Cenozoic

_____ Precambrian

_____ Paleozoic

_____ Mesozoic

3. A scientist finds the fossil of a fern in Antarctica. What can she infer from this discovery? Explain.

_____

_____

_____

Fill in the circle next to the best answer.

4. What is coal made from?

(A) ancient ferns   (C) tar

(B) tree resin   (D) animal bones

Name

Unscramble the letters in bold print to make a word that names a cycle.

1. The phases of the moon make the **runal** cycle.
2. A **feil** cycle describes how an organism grows and reproduces.
3. The **yoxeng** cycle explains how producers and consumers work together to make the air they need to survive.
4. Plants use the cycle of **steshithoopnys** to make sugar they need for energy.
5. Earth revolves around the sun, creating the **aneslaso** cycle.
6. The **tware** cycle involves the condensation and evaporation of water.

Day #1

Write *true* or *false*.

1. _____ The amount of nitrogen changes because of the nitrogen cycle.
2. _____ The proteins in nitrogen promote cell growth and repair.
3. _____ Most organisms cannot use nitrogen gas.
4. _____ Lightning and special kinds of bacteria turn nitrogen compounds into gas.
5. _____ Decomposers restore nitrogen to soil.
6. _____ Nitrogen made by lightning washes into the soil with the help of rain.

Day #2

Draw a line to match each phase with its description. Then, write numbers **1** through **8** to show the correct order of the lunar cycle.

_____ waxing gibbous moon
_____ third-quarter moon
_____ waning gibbous moon
_____ waxing crescent moon
_____ first-quarter moon
_____ waning crescent moon
_____ new moon
_____ full moon

The moon looks like a big, bright circle.
A sliver of the shrinking moon is lit.
A sliver of the growing moon is lit.
One half of the shrinking moon is lit.
The moon looks dark in the night sky.
The growing moon's surface is mostly lit.
One half of the growing moon is lit.
The shrinking moon's surface is mostly lit.

Day #3

Describe the life cycle of a flowering plant. Use the words in the box in your paragraph.

| seedling | pollinate | germinate |

_____
_____
_____
_____

Day #4

Assessment

Assessment # 39

Fill in the circle next to the best answer.

1. Which is not a factor in the rock cycle?

   (A) heat   (C) air

   (B) pressure   (D) erosion

2. Which force affects tides?

   (A) friction   (C) inertia

   (B) gravity   (D) magnetism

3. Which form of energy causes the water cycle?

   (A) static electricity   (C) infrared

   (B) solar   (D) sound

4. Ito sees this flowering plant in the garden. What part of the life cycle does he see?

   (A) seedling   (C) germinating

   (B) seed   (D) pollinating

Answer the question.

5. Many cycles are interrelated. For one cycle to continue, it needs the help of another. Choose two cycles. Tell how they work together. Then, explain why they are important to the balance of nature.

   _____

   _____

   _____

   _____

What do people invent things? Give two reasons.

_____

_____

Name one inventor. Tell what the person invented and why it was useful.

_____

_____

_____

Day #1

At the age of nine, Brandon Whale visited the hospital and saw young children crying when they got shots. Whale discovered that the children's veins were small and hard to locate. Moreover, the veins were even harder to find when the children were anxious and tense. Whale made a soft ball that looked like a beetle. Children could squeeze it, which helped the veins relax. The kids relaxed, too, because they liked to hold the toy. Brandon called his invention the "Needle Beetle." A toy company liked the idea so much that they started to manufacture Whale's invention.

Why did Whale invent the "Needle Beetle"?

_____

Day #2

At the age of eleven, Cassidy Goldstein was doing a school assignment. Many of the crayons she had were broken, so drawing was hard. Goldstein came up with a solution that would hold the broken crayons. Goldstein, using the plastic tube that held water for a single rose, put the crayon in the tube. The holder worked much like a teacher's chalk holder. It was an instant success with the teacher for two reasons. It made small pieces of crayons useable, and children could more easily grip the broken crayons.

Why was Goldstein's invention a good idea? Give two examples.

_____

Day #3

With the help of her father, Cassidy Goldstein patented the "Crayon Holder," which meant that she would keep the right to build and sell the invention. Goldstein now sells the holder through catalogs and in some major stores. Moreover, Goldstein's invention gave her father an idea, too. Mr. Goldstein formed a company that helps kids build, market, and sell their inventions.

How did Cassidy Goldstein's invention help produce another good idea? Explain.

_____

_____

Day #4

Assessment # 40

Fill in the circle next to the best answer.

1. Which could be Brandon Whale's hypothesis for making the Needle Beetle?

   (A) Beetles are cute.

   (B) Children will feel less anxious about shots if they hold something cute.

   (C) Squeezing something makes the veins bigger.

   (D) Crying children are unhappy.

2. Which is a characteristic of a good inventor?

   (A) observant   (C) quick

   (B) happy   (D) selfish

Answer the questions.

3. Is an inventor a scientist? Explain.

_____

_____

_____

_____

4. Many inventions are made to solve a problem. Think of a problem you would like to solve. Design an invention for it. Explain the invention below and tell how it solves the problem.

_____

_____

_____

_____

_____

_____

Answer Key

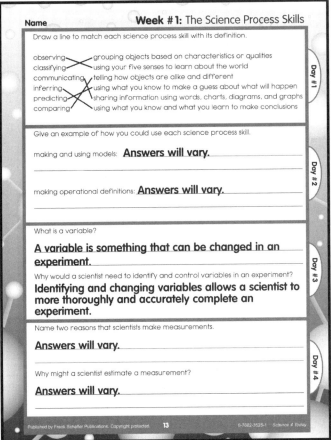

Name _____

Draw a line to match each science process skill with its definition.

observing — grouping objects based on characteristics or qualities
classifying — using your five senses to learn about the world
communicating — telling how objects are alike and different
inferring — using what you know to make a guess about what will happen
predicting — sharing information using words, charts, diagrams, and graphs
comparing — using what you know and what you learn to make conclusions

Give an example of how you could use each science process skill.

making and using models: **Answers will vary.**

making operational definitions: **Answers will vary.**

What is a variable?

A variable is something that can be changed in an experiment.

Why would a scientist need to identify and control variables in an experiment?
Identifying and changing variables allows a scientist to more thoroughly and accurately complete an experiment.

Name two reasons that scientists make measurements.

Answers will vary.

Why might a scientist estimate a measurement?

Answers will vary.

Day #1 _Day #2_ _Day #3_ _Day #4_

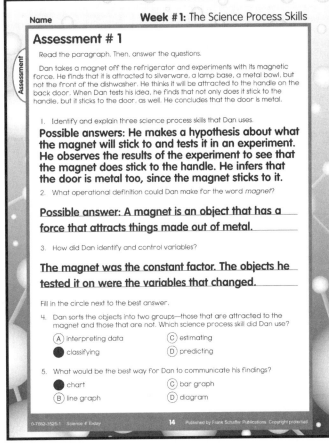

Name _____

Assessment # 1

Read the paragraph. Then, answer the questions.

Dan takes a magnet off the refrigerator and experiments with its magnetic force. He finds that it is attracted to silverware, a lamp base, a metal bowl, but not the front of the dishwasher. He thinks it will be attracted to the handle on the back door. When Dan tests his idea, he finds that not only does it stick to the handle, but it sticks to the door, as well. He concludes that the door is metal.

1. Identify and explain three science process skills that Dan uses.

Possible answers: He makes a hypothesis about what the magnet will stick to and tests it in an experiment. He observes the results of the experiment to see that the magnet does stick to the handle. He infers that the door is metal too, since the magnet sticks to it.

2. What operational definition could Dan make for the word _magnet_?

Possible answer: A magnet is an object that has a force that attracts things made out of metal.

3. How did Dan identify and control variables?

The magnet was the constant factor. The objects he tested it on were the variables that changed.

Fill in the circle next to the best answer.

4. Dan sorts the objects into two groups—those that are attracted to the magnet and those that are not. Which science process skill did Dan use?
   (A) interpreting data   (C) estimating
   ● classifying   (D) predicting

5. What would be the best way for Dan to communicate his findings?
   ● chart   (C) bar graph
   (B) line graph   (D) diagram

Assessment

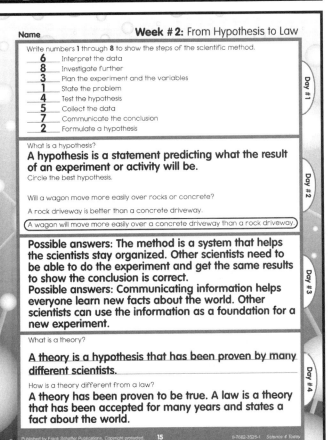

Name _____

Write numbers 1 through 8 to show the steps of the scientific method.

6 Interpret the data
8 Investigate further
3 Plan the experiment and the variables
1 State the problem
4 Test the hypothesis
5 Collect the data
7 Communicate the conclusion
2 Formulate a hypothesis

What is a hypothesis?
A hypothesis is a statement predicting what the result of an experiment or activity will be.
Circle the best hypothesis.

Will a wagon move more easily over rocks or concrete?
A rock driveway is better than a concrete driveway.
(A wagon will move more easily over a concrete driveway than a rock driveway.)

Possible answers: The method is a system that helps the scientists stay organized. Other scientists need to be able to do the experiment and get the same results to show the conclusion is correct.
Possible answers: Communicating information helps everyone learn new facts about the world. Other scientists can use the information as a foundation for a new experiment.

What is a theory?

A theory is a hypothesis that has been proven by many different scientists.

How is a theory different from a law?
A theory has been proven to be true. A law is a theory that has been accepted for many years and states a fact about the world.

Day #1 _Day #2_ _Day #3_ _Day #4_

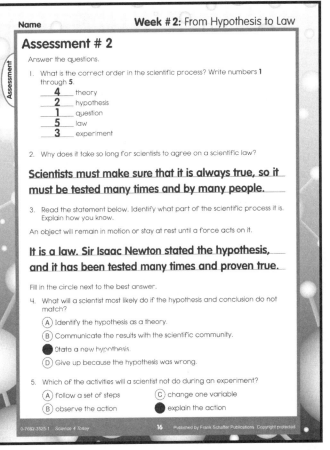

Name _____

Assessment # 2

Answer the questions.

1. What is the correct order in the scientific process? Write numbers 1 through 5.
   4 theory
   2 hypothesis
   1 question
   5 law
   3 experiment

2. Why does it take so long for scientists to agree on a scientific law?

Scientists must make sure that it is always true, so it must be tested many times and by many people.

3. Read the statement below. Identify what part of the scientific process it is. Explain how you know.
An object will remain in motion or stay at rest until a force acts on it.

It is a law. Sir Isaac Newton stated the hypothesis, and it has been tested many times and proven true.

Fill in the circle next to the best answer.

4. What will a scientist most likely do if the hypothesis and conclusion do not match?
   (A) Identify the hypothesis as a theory.
   (B) Communicate the results with the scientific community.
   ● State a new hypothesis.
   (D) Give up because the hypothesis was wrong.

5. Which of the activities will a scientist not do during an experiment?
   (A) follow a set of steps   (C) change one variable
   (B) observe the action   ● explain the action

Assessment

Answer Key

Day #1

Possible answer: The customary system uses feet and inches to measure length, pounds to measure weight, cups to measure capacity, and Fahrenheit degrees to measure temperature.
Possible answer: The metric system is based on tens. It uses centimeters and millimeters to measure length, grams to measure mass, liters to measure volume, and Celsius degrees to measure temperature.

What measurement system is used in the science community?

The metric system is used in the science community.

Why do all scientists use this system?

Possible answer: The metric system allows scientists all around the world to understand the data gathered, even if they do not speak the same language.

Day #2

Mia made a chart to show the kinds of materials in her recycling bin. What two conclusions can she make based on the data in the chart?

Material	Number of Pieces
aluminum	8
tin	2
plastics	3
glass	2
paper	5

Answers will vary.

Day #3

Draw a graphic aid to show the data in the chart above.

Possible answer:

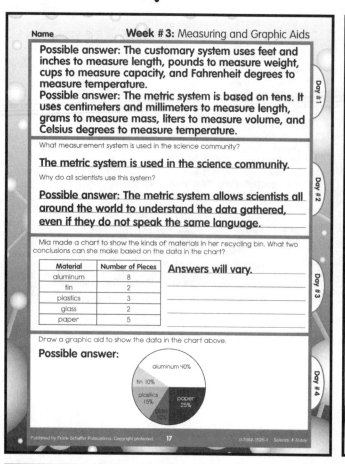

aluminum 40%
tin 10%
plastics 15%
paper 25%
glass 10%

Day #4

Assessment

Assessment # 3

Complete the page.

For an experiment, Carla grew a plant. She measured its growth each week and recorded the data in a chart.

Week	Height (cm)
1	0.5
2	1.0
3	1.5
4	2.0
5	3.0
6	5.0
7	7.0
8	9.0

1. Draw a line graph to show the data.

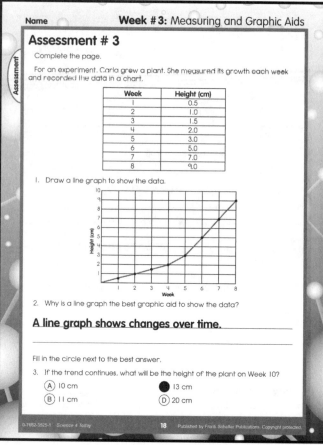

2. Why is a line graph the best graphic aid to show the data?

A line graph shows changes over time.

Fill in the circle next to the best answer.

3. If the trend continues, what will be the height of the plant on Week 10?

(A) 10 cm   ● 13 cm
(B) 11 cm   (D) 20 cm

Day #1

Write *true* or *false*.

1. **true** An experiment always tests a hypothesis.
2. **false** A scientist makes a prediction based on the results of the experiment.
3. **true** Experiments need to be controlled to make sure they are fair.
4. **false** It is important to change at least two variables during an experiment.
5. **true** All data needs to be carefully recorded during an experiment.

Day #2

Should you read through the entire set of instructions before beginning an experiment? Explain.

Possible answer: Yes, you should read the instructions. You need to make sure you have all the materials called for. You also need to know how to set up the experiment to complete it.

Day #3

What are three kinds of clothing people can wear to protect themselves during an experiment?

The clothing includes gloves, goggles, and aprons.

What are three kinds of clothing people should not wear while performing an experiment?

People should not wear loose clothing, dangling jewelry, or opened-toed shoes.

Day #4

What are three safety rules, not related to clothing, that people should follow during an experiment?

Answers will vary.

Assessment

Assessment # 4

Complete the page.

1. Lana noticed that some plants in the backyard were turning yellow. What should Lana do before stating a hypothesis?

Possible answer: She should examine the plant for problems, such as bugs and amounts of water given to the plant.

2. In planning the experiment, what three materials might Lana need?

Possible answers: goggles, hand lens, water

3. Describe an experiment Lana can do to find out why the plants are turning yellow.

Answers will vary.

Answer Key

Week # 5: A Good Scientist

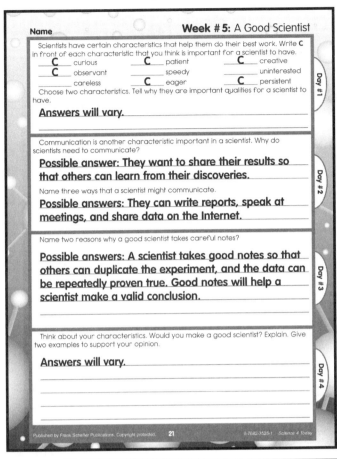

Scientists have certain characteristics that help them do their best work. Write **C** in front of each characteristic that you think is important for a scientist to have.

___**C**___ curious   ___**C**___ patient   ___**C**___ creative
___**C**___ observant   ___ speedy   ___ uninterested
___ careless   ___**C**___ eager   ___**C**___ persistent

Choose two characteristics. Tell why they are important qualities for a scientist to have.

Answers will vary.

Day #1

Communication is another characteristic important in a scientist. Why do scientists need to communicate?

Possible answer: They want to share their results so that others can learn from their discoveries.

Name three ways that a scientist might communicate.

Possible answers: They can write reports, speak at meetings, and share data on the Internet.

Day #2

Name two reasons why a good scientist takes careful notes?

Possible answers: A scientist takes good notes so that others can duplicate the experiment, and the data can be repeatedly proven true. Good notes will help a scientist make a valid conclusion.

Day #3

Think about your characteristics. Would you make a good scientist? Explain. Give two examples to support your opinion.

Answers will vary.

Day #4

Published by Frank Schaffer Publications. Copyright protected.   21   0-7682-3525-1   *Science 4 Today*

Week # 5: A Good Scientist

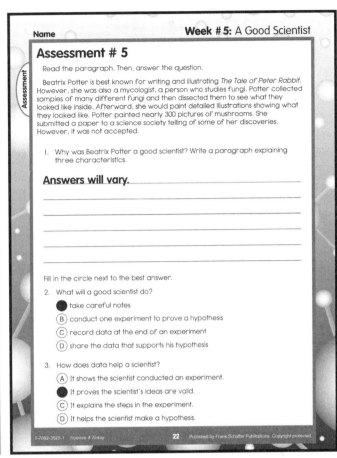

Assessment # 5

Read the paragraph. Then, answer the question.

Beatrix Potter is best known for writing and illustrating *The Tale of Peter Rabbit*. However, she was also a mycologist, a person who studies fungi. Potter collected samples of many different fungi and then dissected them to see what they looked like inside. Afterward, she would paint detailed illustrations showing what they looked like. Potter painted nearly 300 pictures of mushrooms. She submitted a paper to a science society telling of some of her discoveries. However, it was not accepted.

1. Why was Beatrix Potter a good scientist? Write a paragraph explaining three characteristics.

Answers will vary.

Fill in the circle next to the best answer.

2. What will a good scientist do?
   ● take careful notes
   (B) conduct one experiment to prove a hypothesis
   (C) record data at the end of an experiment
   (D) share the data that supports his hypothesis

3. How does data help a scientist?
   (A) It shows the scientist conducted an experiment.
   ● It proves the scientist's ideas are valid.
   (C) It explains the steps in the experiment.
   (D) It helps the scientist make a hypothesis.

0-7682-3525-1   *Science 4 Today*   22   Published by Frank Schaffer Publications. Copyright protected.

Week # 6: Elements

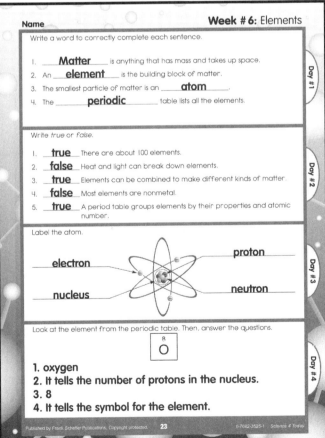

Write a word to correctly complete each sentence.

1. ___**Matter**___ is anything that has mass and takes up space.
2. An ___**element**___ is the building block of matter.
3. The smallest particle of matter is an ___**atom**___.
4. The ___**periodic**___ table lists all the elements.

Day #1

Write *true* or *false*.

1. ___**true**___ There are about 100 elements.
2. ___**false**___ Heat and light can break down elements.
3. ___**true**___ Elements can be combined to make different kinds of matter.
4. ___**false**___ Most elements are nonmetal.
5. ___**true**___ A period table groups elements by their properties and atomic number.

Day #2

Label the atom.

electron   proton
nucleus   neutron

Day #3

Look at the element from the periodic table. Then, answer the questions.

8
O

1. oxygen
2. It tells the number of protons in the nucleus.
3. 8
4. It tells the symbol for the element.

Day #4

Published by Frank Schaffer Publications. Copyright protected.   23   0-7682-3525-1   *Science 4 Today*

Week # 6: Elements

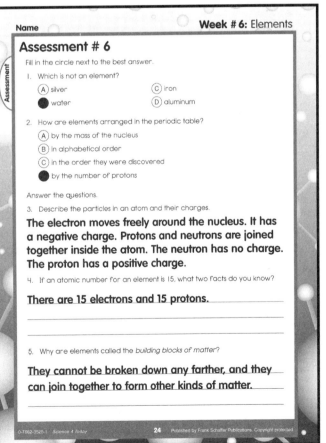

Assessment # 6

Fill in the circle next to the best answer.

1. Which is not an element?
   (A) silver   (C) iron
   ● water   (D) aluminum

2. How are elements arranged in the periodic table?
   (A) by the mass of the nucleus
   (B) in alphabetical order
   (C) in the order they were discovered
   ● by the number of protons

Answer the questions.

3. Describe the particles in an atom and their charges.

The electron moves freely around the nucleus. It has a negative charge. Protons and neutrons are joined together inside the atom. The neutron has no charge. The proton has a positive charge.

4. If an atomic number for an element is 15, what two facts do you know?

There are 15 electrons and 15 protons.

5. Why are elements called the *building blocks of matter*?

They cannot be broken down any farther, and they can join together to form other kinds of matter.

0-7682-3525-1   *Science 4 Today*   24   Published by Frank Schaffer Publications. Copyright protected.

Answer Key

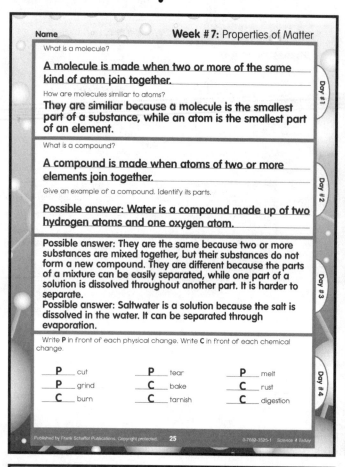

Name

Week # 7: Properties of Matter

What is a molecule?

A molecule is made when two or more of the same kind of atom join together.

How are molecules similiar to atoms?

They are similiar because a molecule is the smallest part of a substance, while an atom is the smallest part of an element.

Day #1

What is a compound?

A compound is made when atoms of two or more elements join together.

Give an example of a compound. Identify its parts.

Possible answer: Water is a compound made up of two hydrogen atoms and one oxygen atom.

Day #2

Possible answer: They are the same because two or more substances are mixed together, but their substances do not form a new compound. They are different because the parts of a mixture can be easily separated, while one part of a solution is dissolved throughout another part. It is harder to separate.
Possible answer: Saltwater is a solution because the salt is dissolved in the water. It can be separated through evaporation.

Day #3

Write **P** in front of each physical change. Write **C** in front of each chemical change.

P cut	**P** tear	**P** melt
P grind	**C** bake	**C** rust
C burn	**C** tarnish	**C** digestion

Day #4

Published by Frank Schaffer Publications. Copyright protected.   25   0-7682-3525-1   *Science 4 Today*

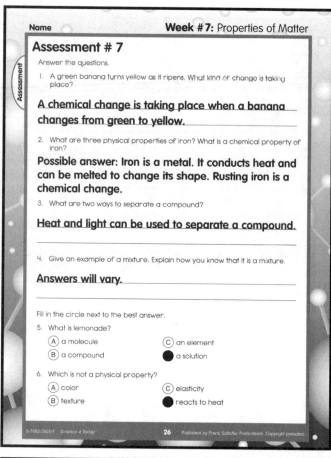

Name   **Week # 7:** Properties of Matter

Assessment

Assessment # 7

Answer the questions.

1. A green banana turns yellow as it ripens. What kind of change is taking place?

A chemical change is taking place when a banana changes from green to yellow.

2. What are three physical properties of iron? What is a chemical property of iron?

Possible answer: Iron is a metal. It conducts heat and can be melted to change its shape. Rusting iron is a chemical change.

3. What are two ways to separate a compound?

Heat and light can be used to separate a compound.

4. Give an example of a mixture. Explain how you know that it is a mixture.

Answers will vary.

Fill in the circle next to the best answer.

5. What is lemonade?
   - (A) a molecule
   - (B) a compound
   - (C) an element
   - ● a solution

6. Which is not a physical property?
   - (A) color
   - (B) texture
   - (C) elasticity
   - ● reacts to heat

0-7682-3525-1   *Science 4 Today*   26   Published by Frank Schaffer Publications. Copyright protected.

Name   **Week # 8:** Motion

What is speed?

Speed is the measure of how far something moves in a set amount of time.

Mrs. Carlos drives 150 kilometers in 2 hours. What is her speed per hour? Explain how you found the answer.

75 km/hr; To find the speed, divide the total number of miles by the time of travel.

Day #1

Write a word to complete each sentence.

1. The tendency for an object to stay at rest or in motion is called **inertia**.
2. A **force** can make something move or cause it to stop.
3. The pull of **gravity** is weaker when two objects are farther apart.
4. The measure of speed in a certain direction is called **velocity**.
5. When a car **accelerates**, its rate of speed changes.

Day #2

Think about riding in a car. What happens to your body when the car stops suddenly? Explain what force is at work.

It keeps moving. The force of inertia is at work because an object will remain in motion unless a force acts on it.

How does an object's mass affect its motion?

Possible answer: The greater an object's mass, the greater the pull of gravity between it and another object.

Day #3

What is friction?

Friction is the force that slows an object's movement.

What are three ways to reduce friction?

Answers will vary.

Day #4

Published by Frank Schaffer Publications. Copyright protected.   27   0-7682-3525-1   *Science 4 Today*

Name   **Week # 8:** Motion

Assessment

Assessment # 8

Answer the questions.

1. Why would you weigh less on the moon?

The mass of the moon is smaller than Earth, so its gravity is weaker. My weight would be less because there is less gravity.

2. Think about kicking a soccer ball into a goal. It flies into the air, drops into the goal, and rolls to a stop. Describe three forces that affect the ball's movement.

Possible answers: The push of the foot is the force that makes the ball move. Gravity causes the ball to fall back toward Earth. The friction of the ground causes the ball to stop.

Fill in the circle next to the best answer.

3. Ada was walking north. She turned left and started walking west. What did Ada change?
   - (A) speed
   - ● velocity
   - (C) inertia
   - (D) acceleration

4. What happens when two balls of different masses are dropped from the same height?
   - (A) Gravity pulls them close together.
   - (B) Their speed is different.
   - (C) The larger ball hits the ground first.
   - ● Their acceleration is the same.

5. Which surface provides the greatest amount of friction?
   - (A) ice
   - ● pebbles
   - (C) grass
   - (D) concrete

0-7682-3525-1   *Science 4 Today*   28   Published by Frank Schaffer Publications. Copyright protected.

Answer Key

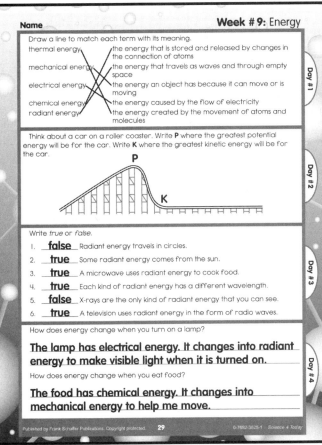

Draw a line to match each term with its meaning.

Day #1

thermal energy		the energy that is stored and released by changes in the connection of atoms
mechanical energy		the energy that travels as waves and through empty space
electrical energy		the energy an object has because it can move or is moving
chemical energy		the energy caused by the flow of electricity
radiant energy		the energy created by the movement of atoms and molecules

Day #2

Think about a car on a roller coaster. Write **P** where the greatest potential energy will be for the car. Write **K** where the greatest kinetic energy will be for the car.

P

K

Day #3

Write *true* or *false*.

1. **false** Radiant energy travels in circles.
2. **true** Some radiant energy comes from the sun.
3. **true** A microwave uses radiant energy to cook food.
4. **true** Each kind of radiant energy has a different wavelength.
5. **false** X-rays are the only kind of radiant energy that you can see.
6. **true** A television uses radiant energy in the form of radio waves.

Day #4

How does energy change when you turn on a lamp?

The lamp has electrical energy. It changes into radiant energy to make visible light when it is turned on.

How does energy change when you eat food?

The food has chemical energy. It changes into mechanical energy to help me move.

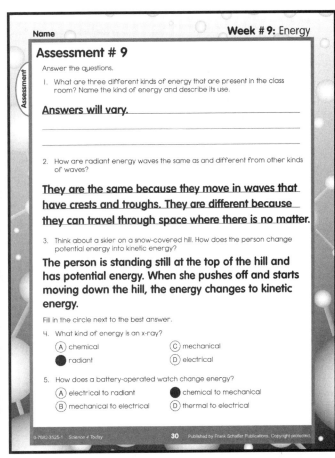

Assessment

Assessment # 9

Answer the questions.

1. What are three different kinds of energy that are present in the class room? Name the kind of energy and describe its use.

Answers will vary.

2. How are radiant energy waves the same as and different from other kinds of waves?

They are the same because they move in waves that have crests and troughs. They are different because they can travel through space where there is no matter.

3. Think about a skier on a snow-covered hill. How does the person change potential energy into kinetic energy?

The person is standing still at the top of the hill and has potential energy. When she pushes off and starts moving down the hill, the energy changes to kinetic energy.

Fill in the circle next to the best answer.

4. What kind of energy is an x-ray?
   - (A) chemical
   - (C) mechanical
   - ● radiant
   - (D) electrical

5. How does a battery-operated watch change energy?
   - (A) electrical to radiant
   - ● chemical to mechanical
   - (B) mechanical to electrical
   - (D) thermal to electrical

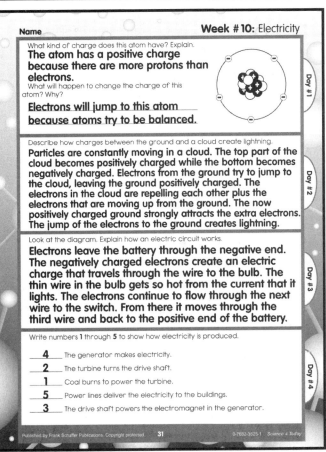

Day #1

What kind of charge does this atom have? Explain.
The atom has a positive charge because there are more protons than electrons.
What will happen to change the charge of this atom? Why?

Electrons will jump to this atom because atoms try to be balanced.

Day #2

Describe how charges between the ground and a cloud create lightning.
Particles are constantly moving in a cloud. The top part of the cloud becomes positively charged while the bottom becomes negatively charged. Electrons from the ground try to jump to the cloud, leaving the ground positively charged. The electrons in the cloud are repelling each other plus the electrons that are moving up from the ground. The now positively charged ground strongly attracts the extra electrons. The jump of the electrons to the ground creates lightning.

Day #3

Look at the diagram. Explain how an electric circuit works.
Electrons leave the battery through the negative end. The negatively charged electrons create an electric charge that travels through the wire to the bulb. The thin wire in the bulb gets so hot from the current that it lights. The electrons continue to flow through the next wire to the switch. From there it moves through the third wire and back to the positive end of the battery.

Day #4

Write numbers 1 through 5 to show how electricity is produced.

- **4** The generator makes electricity.
- **2** The turbine turns the drive shaft.
- **1** Coal burns to power the turbine.
- **5** Power lines deliver the electricity to the buildings.
- **3** The drive shaft powers the electromagnet in the generator.

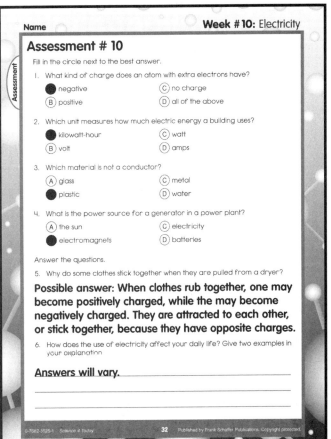

Assessment

Assessment # 10

Fill in the circle next to the best answer.

1. What kind of charge does an atom with extra electrons have?
   - ● negative
   - (C) no charge
   - (B) positive
   - (D) all of the above

2. Which unit measures how much electric energy a building uses?
   - ● kilowatt-hour
   - (C) watt
   - (B) volt
   - (D) amps

3. Which material is not a conductor?
   - (A) glass
   - (C) metal
   - ● plastic
   - (D) water

4. What is the power source for a generator in a power plant?
   - (A) the sun
   - (C) electricity
   - ● electromagnets
   - (D) batteries

Answer the questions.

5. Why do some clothes stick together when they are pulled from a dryer?

Possible answer: When clothes rub together, one may become positively charged, while the may become negatively charged. They are attracted to each other, or stick together, because they have opposite charges.

6. How does the use of electricity affect your daily life? Give two examples in your explanation.

Answers will vary.

Answer Key

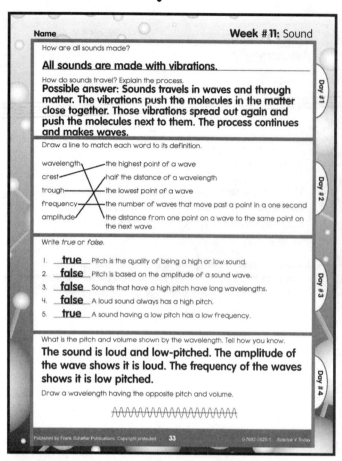

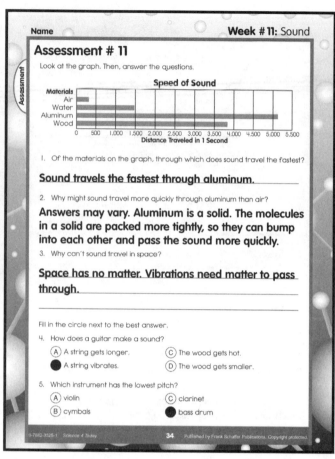

Name **Week # 11:** Sound

Day #1

How are all sounds made?

All sounds are made with vibrations.

How do sounds travel? Explain the process.

Possible answer: Sounds travels in waves and through matter. The vibrations push the molecules in the matter close together. Those vibrations spread out again and push the molecules next to them. The process continues and makes waves.

Day #2

Draw a line to match each word to its definition.

wavelength	the highest point of a wave
crest	half the distance of a wavelength
trough	the lowest point of a wave
frequency	the number of waves that move past a point in a one second
amplitude	the distance from one point on a wave to the same point on the next wave

Day #3

Write *true* or *false*.

1. **true** Pitch is the quality of being a high or low sound.
2. **false** Pitch is based on the amplitude of a sound wave.
3. **false** Sounds that have a high pitch have long wavelengths.
4. **false** A loud sound always has a high pitch.
5. **true** A sound having a low pitch has a low frequency.

Day #4

What is the pitch and volume shown by the wavelength. Tell how you know.

The sound is loud and low-pitched. The amplitude of the wave shows it is loud. The frequency of the waves shows it is low pitched.

Draw a wavelength having the opposite pitch and volume.

Published by Frank Schaffer Publications. Copyright protected. 33 0-7682-3525-1 Science 4 Today

Name **Week # 11:** Sound

Assessment

Assessment # 11

Look at the graph. Then, answer the questions.

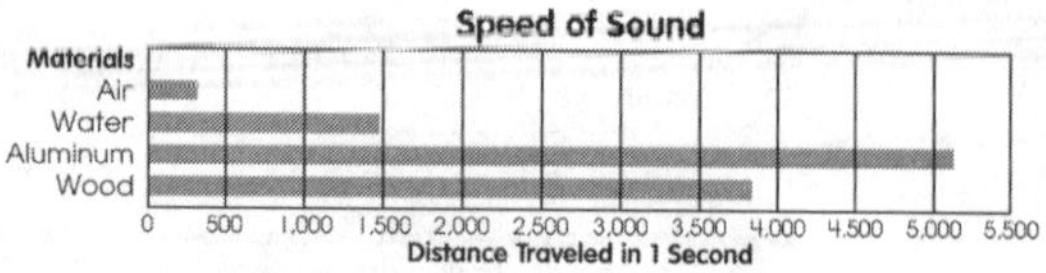

Speed of Sound
Materials
Air
Water
Aluminum
Wood
0 500 1,000 1,500 2,000 2,500 3,000 3,500 4,000 4,500 5,000 5,500
Distance Traveled in 1 Second

1. Of the materials on the graph, through which does sound travel the fastest?

Sound travels the fastest through aluminum.

2. Why might sound travel more quickly through aluminum than air?

Answers may vary. Aluminum is a solid. The molecules in a solid are packed more tightly, so they can bump into each other and pass the sound more quickly.

3. Why can't sound travel in space?

Space has no matter. Vibrations need matter to pass through.

Fill in the circle next to the best answer.

4. How does a guitar make a sound?
   - (A) A string gets longer.
   - ● A string vibrates.
   - (C) The wood gets hot.
   - (D) The wood gets smaller.
5. Which instrument has the lowest pitch?
   - (A) violin
   - (B) cymbals
   - (C) clarinet
   - ● bass drum

0-7682-3525-1 Science 4 Today 34 Published by Frank Schaffer Publications. Copyright protected.

Name **Week # 12:** Classifying

Day #1

Write numbers **1** through **7** to show the order of the scientific classification system from general to specific. Then, write numbers **1** through **7** to show how human beings are classified.

3	class	**1**	Animal
6	genus	**3**	Mammals
1	kingdom	**2**	Vertebrate
7	species	**5**	Carnivore
4	order	**7**	Sapiens
2	phylum	**4**	Primates
5	family	**6**	Homo

Day #2

On the line in front of each kingdom, write one characteristic of those organisms. Then, draw a line to match each kingdom with an organism found in it.

Possible answers:

one cell	Moneran	eagle
cells have a nucleus and other cell parts	Protist	bacteria
absorbs energy from other organisms	Fungus	mushroom
gets energy from the sun	Plant	daisy
gets energy by eating other organisms	Animal	algae

Day #3

Write **C** in front of each characteristic scientists use to classify organisms.

C	cell structure	**C**	how it gets energy
	height	**C**	how it reproduces
	color		how it smells
C	body structure		how it sees

Why do scientists want to classify animals?

Possible answer: They classify organisms to avoid confusion and show how organisms are alike and different.

Day #4

Describe the two main groups of animals.

Vertebrate animals have backbones. Invertebrate animals do not have backbones.

Describe three ways that scientist classify plants.

Scientists classify plants as vascular, or having tubes that carry nutrients and water throughout the plant. They classify them as reproducing by seeds or another way. They also classify by if they flower or not.

Published by Frank Schaffer Publications. Copyright protected. 35 0-7682-3525-1 Science 4 Today

Name **Week # 12:** Classifying

Assessment

Assessment # 12

Answer the questions.

1. How is scientific classification a system?

Possible answer: Organisms are grouped by characteristics in an organized way so that it is easy to understand their relationships to each other.

2. Can two different animals have the same scientific name? Why or why not?

No, because each animal has at least one characteristic that makes it different from every other animal. For that reason, it has a different species name.

3. Describe three characteristics of moss that help scientist classify it.

It is nonvascular and does not have seeds or flowers.

4. Imagine that a new animal has been discovered. It has wings and flies. Its body is covered in fur, and it gives birth to live young, which it feeds milk. How would scientists classify this animal. What animal do you already know about that will help classify it? Explain.

Possible answer: Scientists will classify it as a mammal because it has fur, gives birth to live young, and feeds the young milk. It will be classified closely with a bat because this mammal has wings and flies, too.

Fill in the circle next to the best answer.

5. Which of these is not a characteristic of a mammal?
   - (A) feeds its young milk
   - ● is cold-blooded
   - (C) has fur
   - (D) has a vertebrate

0-7682-3525-1 Science 4 Today 36 Published by Frank Schaffer Publications. Copyright protected.

Answer Key

Day #1

What is a cell?

A cell is the smallest unit in an organism.

List at least four of the six processes of life that cells control?

They control getting energy, using energy, growth, reproduction, waste removal, and response to stimuli.

Day #2

Name the cell. Then, label its parts. Tell what each part does.

Name **Animal Cell**

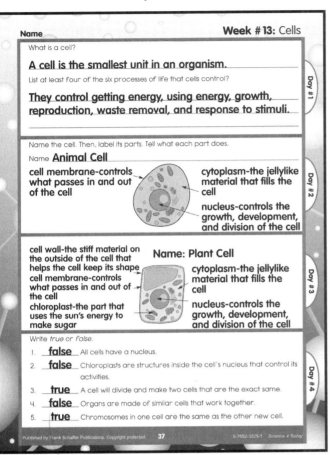

cell membrane-controls what passes in and out of the cell

cytoplasm-the jellylike material that fills the cell

nucleus-controls the growth, development, and division of the cell

Day #3

cell wall-the stiff material on the outside of the cell that helps the cell keep its shape

cell membrane-controls what passes in and out of the cell

chloroplast-the part that uses the sun's energy to make sugar

Name: Plant Cell

cytoplasm-the jellylike material that fills the cell

nucleus-controls the growth, development, and division of the cell

Day #4

Write *true* or *false*.

1. **false** All cells have a nucleus.
2. **false** Chloroplasts are structures inside the cell's nucleus that control its activities.
3. **true** A cell will divide and make two cells that are the exact same.
4. **false** Organs are made of similar cells that work together.
5. **true** Chromosomes in one cell are the same as the other new cell.

Assessment

Assessment # 13

Answer the questions.

1. Identify three specific cells in the human body. Tell what process of life they control.

Answers will vary.

2. Is a virus a kind of cell? Why or why not?

Possible answer: A virus is not a cell because it does not use energy.

3. How do cells help scientists classify animals into kingdoms?

Some kingdoms are made of single-celled organisms, while others are made of multi-celled organisms. Some of the single-celled organisms do not have a nucleus.

4. Describe how cells divide.

The cell makes a copy of its chromosomes. Both sets line up in the middle of the cell. The pair splits and moves to the opposite side of the cell. The cytoplasm and wall divide to make two new cells that are identical.

Fill in the circle next to the best answer.

5. Which of the following is a single cell?
   - ● bacteria
   - Ⓒ heart
   - Ⓑ moss
   - Ⓓ blood

Day #1

Write a word from the box to complete each definition.

| trait | inherit | heredity | reproduction | fertilization | species |

1. **heredity** – the passing of characteristics from one generation to the next
2. **reproduction** – the process of making new organisms
3. **species** – a group of organisms that can reproduce
4. **trait** – a feature or characteristic gotten from a parent
5. **inherit** – to get a characteristic from a parent or ancestor
6. **fertilization** – the process when a sperm cell and egg cell join together

Day #2

What are three traits that organisms in the same species might have?

Possible answers: They might inherit body shape, height, and color of different parts.

What are three specific traits that you inherited from your parents?

Answer will vary.

Day #3

A plant produces both smooth and wrinkled seeds. The smooth seeds are dominant. The wrinkled seeds are recessive. Complete the Punnett square to show what the offspring of these two parent plants will be.

	S	s
S	SS	Ss
s	Ss	ss

Predict what kinds of seed the offspring will have.

The seeds will all be smooth.

Day #4

Unscramble the letters in bold to make words that tell about plant reproduction. Then, write numbers 1 through 6 to tell the order of plant reproduction.

3-pollinates
1-stamen, pistil
4-ovule
6-reproduces
5-fertilizes
2-pollen

Assessment

Assessment # 14

Answer the questions.

1. How does heredity affect a species?

Heredity makes sure that certain traits are passed down in a species so they can survive in the habitat.

2. What are two ways that cells produce new organisms?

One-celled organisms split in two to reproduce. Multi-celled organisms reproduce by joining an egg cell and a sperm cell to create a fertilized egg.

3. What are three factors affecting the growth and development of an organism?

Possible answer: Inherited traits from a parent, such as eye color, greatly affect an organism. There are inherited traits that are affected by the body systems and environment, such as height. There are acquired skills, like playing an instrument, also affect the development of an organism.

4. Suppose one parent has brown eyes and another parent has blue eyes. Which color is dominant? **Brown is dominant.**

5. What combinations of genes might the parents describe above have? Use a capital **B** for dominant and lower case **b** for recessive. (Hint: There may be more than one.)

brown eyes **BB, Bb**

	B	b
B	BB	Bb
b	Bb	bb

blue eyes **bb**

	b	b
B	Bb	Bb
b	bb	bb

Answer Key

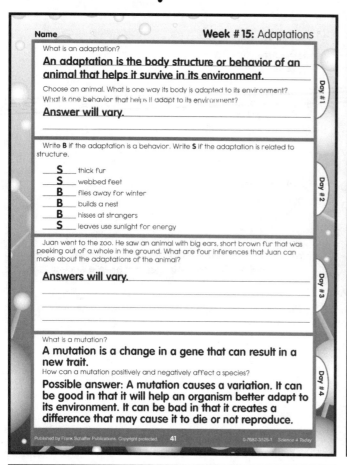

What is an adaptation?

An adaptation is the body structure or behavior of an animal that helps it survive in its environment.

Choose an animal. What is one way its body is adapted to its environment? What is one behavior that helps it adapt to its environment?

Answer will vary.

Day #1

Write **B** if the adaptation is a behavior. Write **S** if the adaptation is related to structure.

S thick fur
S webbed feet
B flies away for winter
B builds a nest
B hisses at strangers
S leaves use sunlight for energy

Day #2

Juan went to the zoo. He saw an animal with big ears, short brown fur that was peeking out of a whole in the ground. What are four inferences that Juan can make about the adaptations of the animal?

Answers will vary.

Day #3

What is a mutation?
A mutation is a change in a gene that can result in a new trait.
How can a mutation positively and negatively affect a species?
Possible answer: A mutation causes a variation. It can be good in that it will help an organism better adapt to its environment. It can be bad in that it creates a difference that may cause it to die or not reproduce.

Day #4

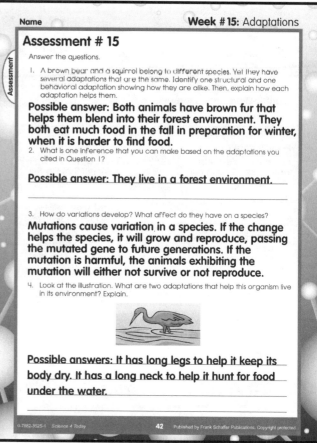

Assessment

Assessment # 15

Answer the questions.

1. A brown bear and a squirrel belong to different species. Yet they have several adaptations that are the same. Identify one structural and one behavioral adaptation showing how they are alike. Then, explain how each adaptation helps them.

Possible answer: Both animals have brown fur that helps them blend into their forest environment. They both eat much food in the fall in preparation for winter, when it is harder to find food.

2. What is one inference that you can make based on the adaptations you cited in Question 1?

Possible answer: They live in a forest environment.

3. How do variations develop? What affect do they have on a species?

Mutations cause variation in a species. If the change helps the species, it will grow and reproduce, passing the mutated gene to future generations. If the mutation is harmful, the animals exhibiting the mutation will either not survive or not reproduce.

4. Look at the illustration. What are two adaptations that help this organism live in its environment? Explain.

Possible answers: It has long legs to help it keep its body dry. It has a long neck to help it hunt for food under the water.

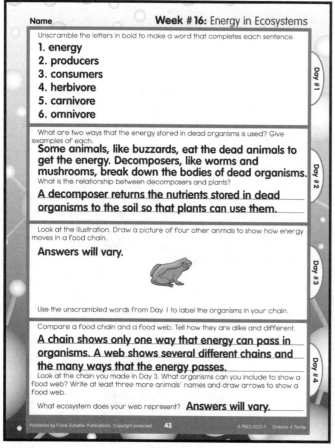

Unscramble the letters in bold to make a word that completes each sentence.

1. **energy**
2. **producers**
3. **consumers**
4. **herbivore**
5. **carnivore**
6. **omnivore**

Day #1

What are two ways that the energy stored in dead organisms is used? Give examples of each.
Some animals, like buzzards, eat the dead animals to get the energy. Decomposers, like worms and mushrooms, break down the bodies of dead organisms.
What is the relationship between decomposers and plants?
A decomposer returns the nutrients stored in dead organisms to the soil so that plants can use them.

Day #2

Look at the illustration. Draw a picture of four other animals to show how energy moves in a food chain.

Answers will vary.

Use the unscrambled words from Day 1 to label the organisms in your chain.

Day #3

Compare a food chain and a food web. Tell how they are alike and different.
A chain shows only one way that energy can pass in organisms. A web shows several different chains and the many ways that the energy passes.
Look at the chain you made in Day 3. What organisms can you include to show a food web? Write at least three more animals' names and draw arrows to show a food web.

What ecosystem does your web represent? **Answers will vary.**

Day #4

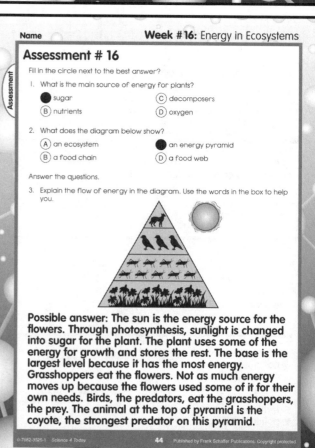

Assessment

Assessment # 16

Fill in the circle next to the best answer?

1. What is the main source of energy for plants?
   ● sugar   (C) decomposers
   (B) nutrients   (D) oxygen

2. What does the diagram below show?
   (A) an ecosystem   ● an energy pyramid
   (B) a food chain   (D) a food web

Answer the questions.

3. Explain the flow of energy in the diagram. Use the words in the box to help you.

Possible answer: The sun is the energy source for the flowers. Through photosynthesis, sunlight is changed into sugar for the plant. The plant uses some of the energy for growth and stores the rest. The base is the largest level because it has the most energy. Grasshoppers eat the flowers. Not as much energy moves up because the flowers used some of it for their own needs. Birds, the predators, eat the grasshoppers, the prey. The animal at the top of pyramid is the coyote, the strongest predator on this pyramid.

Answer Key

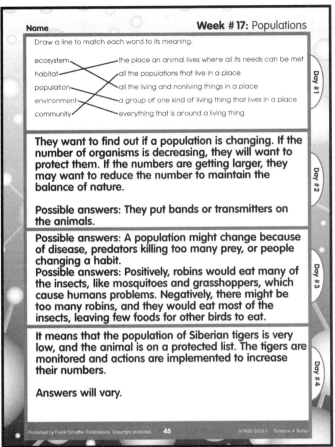

Name _____ **Week #17:** Populations

Draw a line to match each word to its meaning.

ecosystem — the place an animal lives where all its needs can be met
habitat — all the populations that live in a place
population — all the living and nonliving things in a place
environment — a group of one kind of living thing that lives in a place
community — everything that is around a living thing

Day #1

They want to find out if a population is changing. If the number of organisms is decreasing, they will want to protect them. If the numbers are getting larger, they may want to reduce the number to maintain the balance of nature.

Possible answers: They put bands or transmitters on the animals.

Day #2

Possible answers: A population might change because of disease, predators killing too many prey, or people changing a habit.
Possible answers: Positively, robins would eat many of the insects, like mosquitoes and grasshoppers, which cause humans problems. Negatively, there might be too many robins, and they would eat most of the insects, leaving few foods for other birds to eat.

Day #3

It means that the population of Siberian tigers is very low, and the animal is on a protected list. The tigers are monitored and actions are implemented to increase their numbers.

Answers will vary.

Day #4

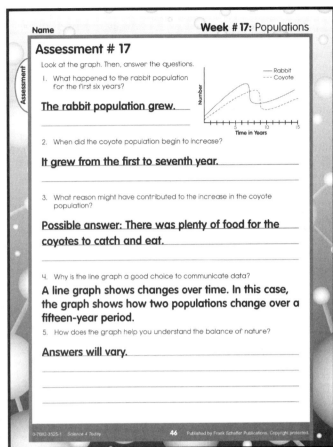

Name _____ **Week #17:** Populations

Assessment # 17

Look at the graph. Then, answer the questions.

1. What happened to the rabbit population for the first six years?

The rabbit population grew.

2. When did the coyote population begin to increase?

It grew from the first to seventh year.

3. What reason might have contributed to the increase in the coyote population?

Possible answer: There was plenty of food for the coyotes to catch and eat.

4. Why is the line graph a good choice to communicate data?

A line graph shows changes over time. In this case, the graph shows how two populations change over a fifteen-year period.

5. How does the graph help you understand the balance of nature?

Answers will vary.

Assessment

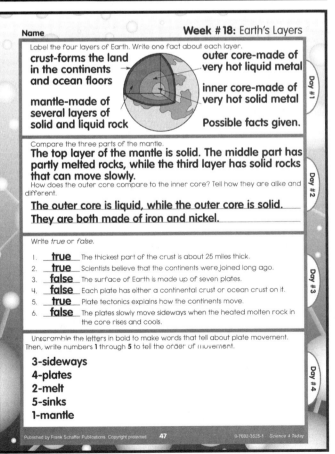

Name _____ **Week #18:** Earth's Layers

Label the four layers of Earth. Write one fact about each layer.

crust-forms the land in the continents and ocean floors

outer core-made of very hot liquid metal

inner core-made of very hot solid metal

mantle-made of several layers of solid and liquid rock

Possible facts given.

Day #1

Compare the three parts of the mantle.
The top layer of the mantle is solid. The middle part has partly melted rocks, while the third layer has solid rocks that can move slowly.
How does the outer core compare to the inner core? Tell how they are alike and different.

The outer core is liquid, while the outer core is solid. They are both made of iron and nickel.

Day #2

Write true or false.
1. **true** The thickest part of the crust is about 25 miles thick.
2. **true** Scientists believe that the continents were joined long ago.
3. **false** The surface of Earth is made up of seven plates.
4. **false** Each plate has either a continental crust or ocean crust on it.
5. **true** Plate tectonics explains how the continents move.
6. **false** The plates slowly move sideways when the heated molten rock in the core rises and cools.

Day #3

Unscramble the letters in bold to make words that tell about plate movement. Then, write numbers 1 through 5 to tell the order of movement.

3-sideways
4-plates
2-melt
5-sinks
1-mantle

Day #4

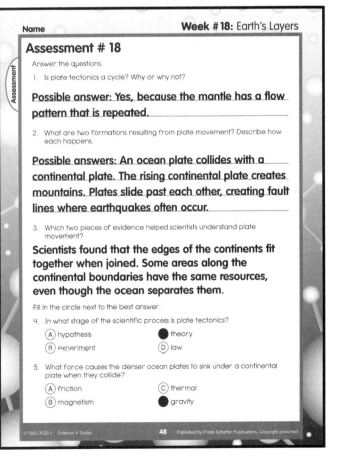

Name _____ **Week #18:** Earth's Layers

Assessment # 18

Answer the questions.

1. Is plate tectonics a cycle? Why or why not?

Possible answer: Yes, because the mantle has a flow pattern that is repeated.

2. What are two formations resulting from plate movement? Describe how each happens.

Possible answers: An ocean plate collides with a continental plate. The rising continental plate creates mountains. Plates slide past each other, creating fault lines where earthquakes often occur.

3. Which two pieces of evidence helped scientists understand plate movement?

Scientists found that the edges of the continents fit together when joined. Some areas along the continental boundaries have the same resources, even though the ocean separates them.

Fill in the circle next to the best answer.

4. In what stage of the scientific process is plate tectonics?
   - (A) hypothesis
   - ● theory
   - (B) experiment
   - (D) law

5. What force causes the denser ocean plates to sink under a continental plate when they collide?
   - (A) friction
   - (C) thermal
   - (B) magnetism
   - ● gravity

Assessment

Answer Key

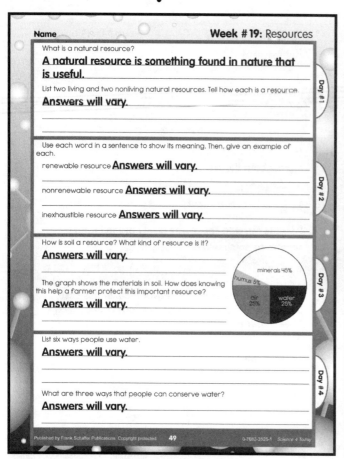

Week #19: Resources

Name

What is a natural resource?

A natural resource is something found in nature that is useful.

List two living and two nonliving natural resources. Tell how each is a resource.
Answers will vary.

Day #1

Use each word in a sentence to show its meaning. Then, give an example of each.

renewable resource **Answers will vary.**

nonrenewable resource **Answers will vary.**

inexhaustible resource **Answers will vary.**

Day #2

How is soil a resource? What kind of resource is it?
Answers will vary.

The graph shows the materials in soil. How does knowing this help a farmer protect this important resource?
Answers will vary.

minerals 45%
humus 5%
air 25%
water 25%

Day #3

List six ways people use water.
Answers will vary.

What are three ways that people can conserve water?
Answers will vary.

Day #4

Name

Week #19: Resources

Assessment

Assessment # 19

Fill in the circle next to the best answer.

1. Which is a fossil fuel?
   - ● petroleum
   - Ⓒ iron
   - Ⓑ aluminum
   - Ⓓ oxygen

2. Which is an inexhaustible resource?
   - Ⓐ trees
   - Ⓒ soil
   - ● wind
   - Ⓓ natural gas

Answer the questions.

3. Can a renewable resource ever be an inexhaustible resource? Explain.

Possible answer: Yes, if monitored and conserved, some renewable resources can be inexhaustible. For example, lumber companies cut trees and replant them. If they continue the process, trees can be an inexhaustible resource.

4. Scientists estimate that the world's supply of petroleum is running out quickly. How will this impact you? How will this impact society? Should people promote stronger conservation measures to slow the loss of this resource? Write a paragraph discussing your opinions.

Answers will vary.

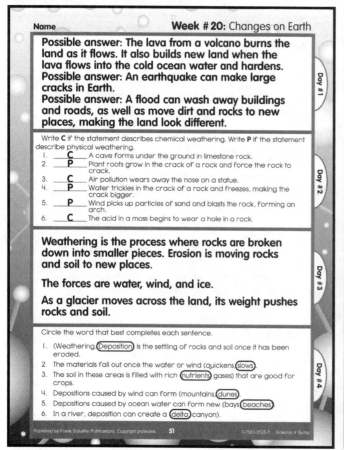

Name

Week #20: Changes on Earth

Possible answer: The lava from a volcano burns the land as it flows. It also builds new land when the lava flows into the cold ocean water and hardens.
Possible answer: An earthquake can make large cracks in Earth.
Possible answer: A flood can wash away buildings and roads, as well as move dirt and rocks to new places, making the land look different.

Day #1

Write **C** if the statement describes chemical weathering. Write **P** if the statement describe physical weathering.

1. **C** A cave forms under the ground in limestone rock.
2. **P** Plant roots grow in the crack of a rock and force the rock to crack.
3. **C** Air pollution wears away the nose on a statue.
4. **P** Water trickles in the crack of a rock and freezes, making the crack bigger.
5. **P** Wind picks up particles of sand and blasts the rock, forming an arch.
6. **C** The acid in a moss begins to wear a hole in a rock.

Day #2

Weathering is the process where rocks are broken down into smaller pieces. Erosion is moving rocks and soil to new places.

The forces are water, wind, and ice.

As a glacier moves across the land, its weight pushes rocks and soil.

Day #3

Circle the word that best completes each sentence.

1. (Weathering, **Deposition**) is the settling of rocks and soil once it has been eroded.
2. The materials fall out once the water or wind (quickens, **slows**).
3. The soil in these areas is filled with rich (**nutrients**, gases) that are good for crops.
4. Depositions caused by wind can form (mountains, **dunes**).
5. Depositions caused by ocean water can form new (bays, **beaches**).
6. In a river, deposition can create a (**delta**, canyon).

Day #4

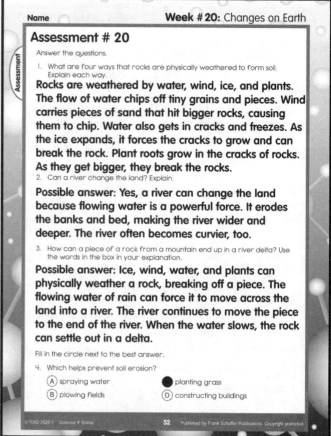

Name

Week #20: Changes on Earth

Assessment

Assessment # 20

Answer the questions.

1. What are four ways that rocks are physically weathered to form soil. Explain each way.

Rocks are weathered by water, wind, ice, and plants. The flow of water chips off tiny grains and pieces. Wind carries pieces of sand that hit bigger rocks, causing them to chip. Water also gets in cracks and freezes. As the ice expands, it forces the cracks to grow and can break the rock. Plant roots grow in the cracks of rocks. As they get bigger, they break the rocks.

2. Can a river change the land? Explain.

Possible answer: Yes, a river can change the land because flowing water is a powerful force. It erodes the banks and bed, making the river wider and deeper. The river often becomes curvier, too.

3. How can a piece of a rock from a mountain end up in a river delta? Use the words in the box in your explanation.

Possible answer: Ice, wind, water, and plants can physically weather a rock, breaking off a piece. The flowing water of rain can force it to move across the land into a river. The river continues to move the piece to the end of the river. When the water slows, the rock can settle out in a delta.

Fill in the circle next to the best answer.

4. Which helps prevent soil erosion?
   - Ⓐ spraying water
   - ● planting grass
   - Ⓑ plowing fields
   - Ⓓ constructing buildings

Answer Key

Write words from the box to complete each statement.

Day #1

1. **atmosphere**
2. **gravity**
3. **troposphere**
4. **exosphere**
5. **stratosphere**
6. **thermosphere**
7. **mesosphere**

Label the diagram. Use the words from Day 1 to help you.

Day #2

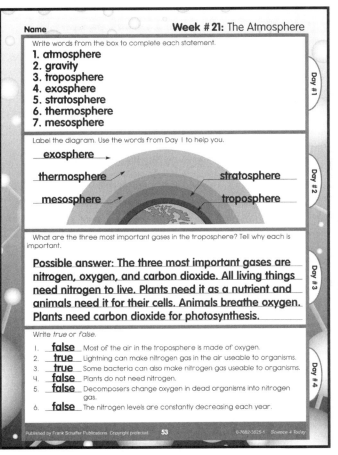

exosphere

thermosphere   **stratosphere**

mesosphere   **troposphere**

What are the three most important gases in the troposphere? Tell why each is important.

Day #3

Possible answer: The three most important gases are nitrogen, oxygen, and carbon dioxide. All living things need nitrogen to live. Plants need it as a nutrient and animals need it for their cells. Animals breathe oxygen. Plants need carbon dioxide for photosynthesis.

Write true or false.

Day #4

1. **false** Most of the air in the troposphere is made of oxygen.
2. **true** Lightning can make nitrogen gas in the air useable to organisms.
3. **true** Some bacteria can also make nitrogen gas useable to organisms.
4. **false** Plants do not need nitrogen.
5. **false** Decomposers change oxygen in dead organisms into nitrogen gas.
6. **false** The nitrogen levels are constantly decreasing each year.

Assessment # 21

Answer the questions.

1. A farmer rotates planting clover and corn in a field each year. Why does he do this? What role does the atmosphere have in the process?

Clover is one plant that has bacteria in its roots that can change nitrogen gas from the atmosphere into a form it can use. The nitrogen goes into the soil to improve the corn crop. Without the nitrogen in the atmosphere, the cycle would not be possible.

2. In what layer will you find ozone gas? Why is this gas important?

The ozone is in the stratosphere. Ozone keeps much of the sun's radiation from reaching the surface of Earth.

3.

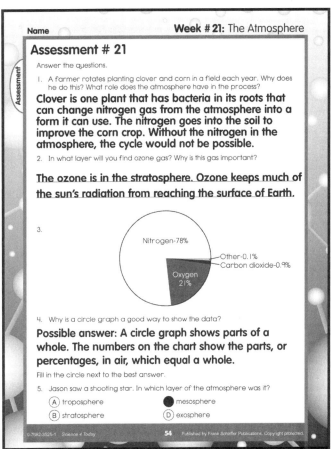

Nitrogen-78%
Other-0.1%
Carbon dioxide-0.9%
Oxygen 21%

4. Why is a circle graph a good way to show the data?

Possible answer: A circle graph shows parts of a whole. The numbers on the chart show the parts, or percentages, in air, which equal a whole.

Fill in the circle next to the best answer.

5. Jason saw a shooting star. In which layer of the atmosphere was it?
   - (A) troposphere
   - ● mesosphere
   - (B) stratosphere
   - (D) exosphere

What is the temperature shown on the thermometer? **18°C**

Day #1

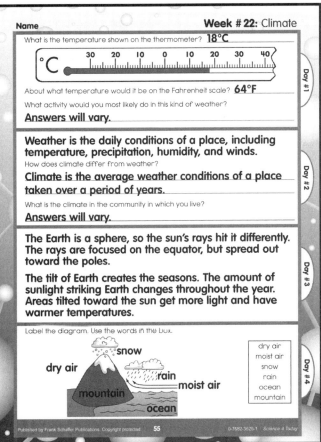

About what temperature would it be on the Fahrenheit scale? **64°F**

What activity would you most likely do in this kind of weather?

Answers will vary.

Day #2

Weather is the daily conditions of a place, including temperature, precipitation, humidity, and winds.

How does climate differ from weather?

Climate is the average weather conditions of a place taken over a period of years.

What is the climate in the community in which you live?

Answers will vary.

Day #3

The Earth is a sphere, so the sun's rays hit it differently. The rays are focused on the equator, but spread out toward the poles.

The tilt of Earth creates the seasons. The amount of sunlight striking Earth changes throughout the year. Areas tilted toward the sun get more light and have warmer temperatures.

Label the diagram. Use the words in the box.

Day #4

snow
dry air
rain
moist air
mountain
ocean

dry air
moist air
snow
rain
ocean
mountain

Assessment # 22

Answer the questions.

1. What is one natural event and one human activity that can affect climate? How does this impact the balance of nature?

Possible answer: An erupting volcano is a natural event that affects climate. Smoke and ash fill the air, blocking the sun and cooling temperatures. Human beings burning fossil fuels for travel and power create more gases in the air. The gases are trapped in the troposphere and heat the air in a process called "the greenhouse effect."

2. The chart below shows the average monthly temperatures and rainfall in Austin, Texas. Use the data to make a line graph of the temperatures.

Month	Temperature (°F)	Precipitation (in.)
Jan.	60	1.9
Feb.	65	2.0
Mar.	73	2.1
Apr.	79	2.5
May	85	5.0
June	91	3.8
July	95	2.0
Aug.	96	2.3
Sept.	90	2.9
Oct.	81	4.0
Nov.	70	2.7
Dec.	62	2.4

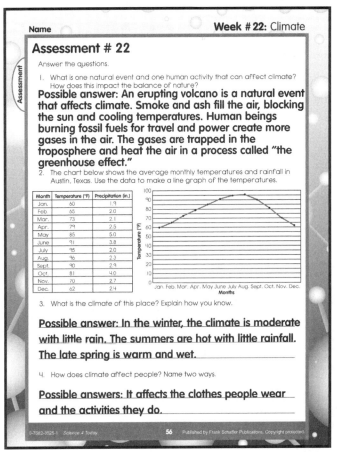

3. What is the climate of this place? Explain how you know.

Possible answer: In the winter, the climate is moderate with little rain. The summers are hot with little rainfall. The late spring is warm and wet.

4. How does climate affect people? Name two ways.

Possible answers: It affects the clothes people wear and the activities they do.

Answer Key

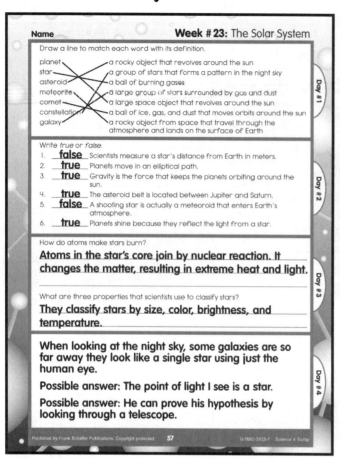

Name **Week # 23:** The Solar System

Day #1

Draw a line to match each word with its definition.

planet — a rocky object that revolves around the sun
star — a group of stars that forms a pattern in the night sky
asteroid — a ball of burning gases
meteorite — a large group of stars surrounded by gas and dust
comet — a large space object that revolves around the sun
constellation — a ball of ice, gas, and dust that moves orbits around the sun
galaxy — a rocky object from space that travel through the atmosphere and lands on the surface of Earth

Day #2

Write *true* or *false*.
1. **false** Scientists measure a star's distance from Earth in meters.
2. **true** Planets move in an elliptical path.
3. **true** Gravity is the force that keeps the planets orbiting around the sun.
4. **true** The asteroid belt is located between Jupiter and Saturn.
5. **false** A shooting star is actually a meteoroid that enters Earth's atmosphere.
6. **true** Planets shine because they reflect the light from a star.

Day #3

How do atoms make stars burn?
Atoms in the star's core join by nuclear reaction. It changes the matter, resulting in extreme heat and light.

What are three properties that scientists use to classify stars?
They classify stars by size, color, brightness, and temperature.

Day #4

When looking at the night sky, some galaxies are so far away they look like a single star using just the human eye.
Possible answer: The point of light I see is a star.
Possible answer: He can prove his hypothesis by looking through a telescope.

Published by Frank Schaffer Publications. Copyright protected.   57   0-7682-3525-1   Science 4 Today

---

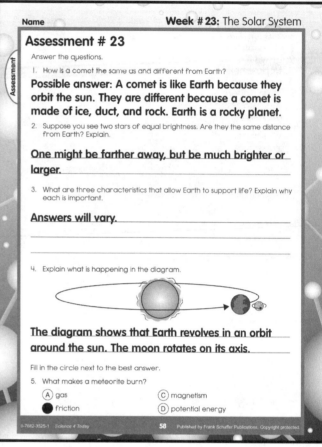

Name **Week # 23:** The Solar System

Assessment

Assessment # 23

Answer the questions.

1. How is a comet the same as and different from Earth?
Possible answer: A comet is like Earth because they orbit the sun. They are different because a comet is made of ice, duct, and rock. Earth is a rocky planet.

2. Suppose you see two stars of equal brightness. Are they the same distance from Earth? Explain.
One might be farther away, but be much brighter or larger.

3. What are three characteristics that allow Earth to support life? Explain why each is important.
Answers will vary.

4. Explain what is happening in the diagram.

The diagram shows that Earth revolves in an orbit around the sun. The moon rotates on its axis.

Fill in the circle next to the best answer.
5. What makes a meteorite burn?
Ⓐ gas   Ⓒ magnetism
● friction   Ⓓ potential energy

0-7682-3525-1   Science 4 Today   58   Published by Frank Schaffer Publications. Copyright protected.

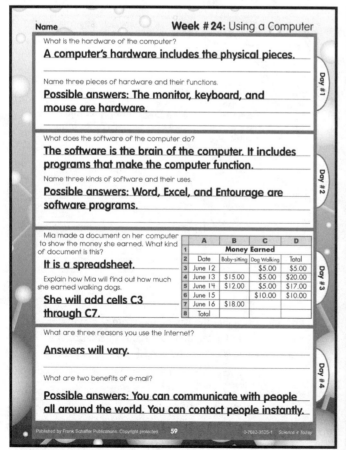

Name **Week # 24:** Using a Computer

Day #1

What is the hardware of the computer?
A computer's hardware includes the physical pieces.

Name three pieces of hardware and their functions.
Possible answers: The monitor, keyboard, and mouse are hardware.

Day #2

What does the software of the computer do?
The software is the brain of the computer. It includes programs that make the computer function.

Name three kinds of software and their uses.
Possible answers: Word, Excel, and Entourage are software programs.

Day #3

Mia made a document on her computer to show the money she earned. What kind of document is this?
It is a spreadsheet.

Explain how Mia will find out how much she earned walking dogs.
She will add cells C3 through C7.

	A	B	C	D
1		Money Earned		
2	Date	Baby-sitting	Dog Walking	Total
3	June 12		$5.00	$5.00
4	June 13	$15.00	$5.00	$20.00
5	June 14	$12.00	$5.00	$17.00
6	June 15		$10.00	$10.00
7	June 16	$18.00		
8	Total			

Day #4

What are three reasons you use the Internet?
Answers will vary.

What are two benefits of e-mail?
Possible answers: You can communicate with people all around the world. You can contact people instantly.

Published by Frank Schaffer Publications. Copyright protected.   59   0-7682-3525-1   Science 4 Today

---

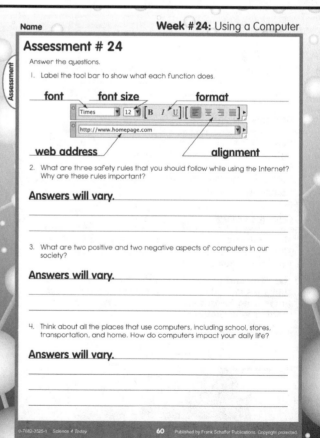

Name **Week # 24:** Using a Computer

Assessment

Assessment # 24

Answer the questions.

1. Label the tool bar to show what each function does.

font   font size   format
web address   alignment

2. What are three safety rules that you should follow while using the Internet? Why are these rules important?
Answers will vary.

3. What are two positive and two negative aspects of computers in our society?
Answers will vary.

4. Think about all the places that use computers, including school, stores, transportation, and home. How do computers impact your daily life?
Answers will vary.

0-7682-3525-1   Science 4 Today   60   Published by Frank Schaffer Publications. Copyright protected.

0-7682-3525-1   *Science 4 Today*   **104**   Published by Frank Schaffer Publications. Copyright protected.

Answer Key

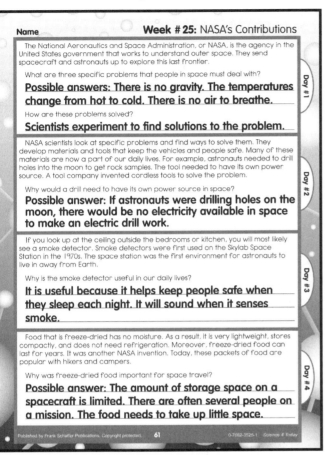

Day #1

The National Aeronautics and Space Administration, or NASA, is the agency in the United States government that works to understand outer space. They send spacecraft and astronauts up to explore this last frontier.

What are three specific problems that people in space must deal with?

Possible answers: There is no gravity. The temperatures change from hot to cold. There is no air to breathe.

How are these problems solved?

Scientists experiment to find solutions to the problem.

Day #2

NASA scientists look at specific problems and find ways to solve them. They develop materials and tools that keep the vehicles and people safe. Many of these materials are now a part of our daily lives. For example, astronauts needed to drill holes into the moon to get rock samples. The tool needed to have its own power source. A tool company invented cordless tools to solve the problem.

Why would a drill need to have its own power source in space?

Possible answer: If astronauts were drilling holes on the moon, there would be no electricity available in space to make an electric drill work.

Day #3

If you look up at the ceiling outside the bedrooms or kitchen, you will most likely see a smoke detector. Smoke detectors were first used on the Skylab Space Station in the 1970s. The space station was the first environment for astronauts to live in away from Earth.

Why is the smoke detector useful in our daily lives?

It is useful because it helps keep people safe when they sleep each night. It will sound when it senses smoke.

Day #4

Food that is freeze-dried has no moisture. As a result, it is very lightweight, stores compactly, and does not need refrigeration. Moreover, freeze-dried food can last for years. It was another NASA invention. Today, these packets of food are popular with hikers and campers.

Why was freeze-dried food important for space travel?

Possible answer: The amount of storage space on a spacecraft is limited. There are often several people on a mission. The food needs to take up little space.

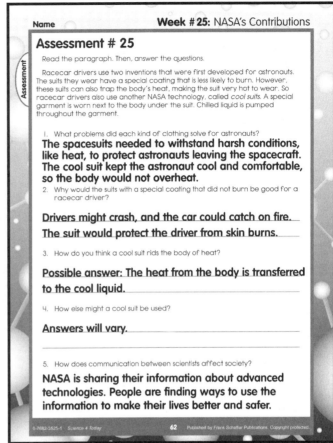

Assessment # 25

Read the paragraph. Then, answer the questions.

Racecar drivers use two inventions that were first developed for astronauts. The suits they wear have a special coating that is less likely to burn. However, these suits can also trap the body's heat, making the suit very hot to wear. So racecar drivers also use another NASA technology, called *cool suits*. A special garment is worn next to the body under the suit. Chilled liquid is pumped throughout the garment.

1. What problems did each kind of clothing solve for astronauts?

The spacesuits needed to withstand harsh conditions, like heat, to protect astronauts leaving the spacecraft. The cool suit kept the astronaut cool and comfortable, so the body would not overheat.

2. Why would the suits with a special coating that did not burn be good for a racecar driver?

Drivers might crash, and the car could catch on fire. The suit would protect the driver from skin burns.

3. How do you think a cool suit rids the body of heat?

Possible answer: The heat from the body is transferred to the cool liquid.

4. How else might a cool suit be used?

Answers will vary.

5. How does communication between scientists affect society?

NASA is sharing their information about advanced technologies. People are finding ways to use the information to make their lives better and safer.

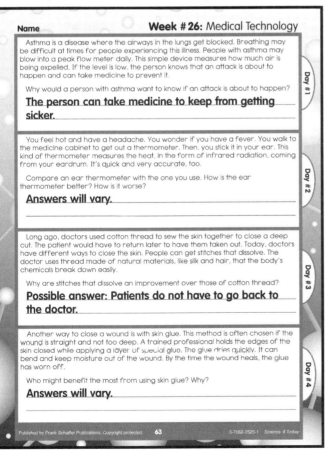

Day #1

Asthma is a disease where the airways in the lungs get blocked. Breathing may be difficult at times for people experiencing this illness. People with asthma may blow into a peak flow meter daily. This simple device measures how much air is being expelled. If the level is low, the person knows that an attack is about to happen and can take medicine to prevent it.

Why would a person with asthma want to know if an attack is about to happen?

The person can take medicine to keep from getting sicker.

Day #2

You feel hot and have a headache. You wonder if you have a fever. You walk to the medicine cabinet to get out a thermometer. Then, you stick it in your ear. This kind of thermometer measures the heat, in the form of infrared radiation, coming from your eardrum. It's quick and very accurate, too.

Compare an ear thermometer with the one you use. How is the ear thermometer better? How is it worse?

Answers will vary.

Day #3

Long ago, doctors used cotton thread to sew the skin together to close a deep cut. The patient would have to return later to have them taken out. Today, doctors have different ways to close the skin. People can get stitches that dissolve. The doctor uses thread made of natural materials, like silk and hair, that the body's chemicals break down easily.

Why are stitches that dissolve an improvement over those of cotton thread?

Possible answer: Patients do not have to go back to the doctor.

Day #4

Another way to close a wound is with skin glue. This method is often chosen if the wound is straight and not too deep. A trained professional holds the edges of the skin closed while applying a layer of special glue. The glue dries quickly. It can bend and keep moisture out of the wound. By the time the wound heals, the glue has worn off.

Who might benefit the most from using skin glue? Why?

Answers will vary.

Assessment # 26

Read the paragraph. Then, answer the questions.

Jon Comer is a professional skateboarder who attends competitions around the world. He drops into a half-pipe and does many amazing tricks. What is really amazing is that Comer has an artificial limb, called a *prosthetic*, on one leg. Scientists join technology and science to help many people like Comer. The limbs are made of a kind of flexible plastics with a microprocessor inside. When joined to the body, muscle movement is changed to electric signals, which makes the artificial limb move.

1. What do you think the microprocessor does in prosthetics?

It is the part that reads the muscle movement and sends the signals telling the limb how to move.

2. Why is it important that science and technology work together? Give three reasons.

Answers will vary.

Answer Key

Name
Week # 27: Telescopes

What is a telescope? How does it work?

A telescope is a tool that makes distance objects look closer. It uses mirrors and lenses to bend and focus light.

How is an optical telescope different from a radio telescope?

Optical telescopes only collect images that use visible light. Radio telescopes use radio waves. They do not need light, so can gather information about objects that are invisible to the human eye.

Label the lens. Draw lines to show how light moves through it. Then, describe the movement.

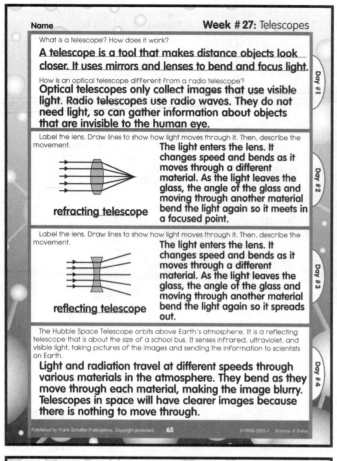

refracting telescope

The light enters the lens. It changes speed and bends as it moves through a different material. As the light leaves the glass, the angle of the glass and moving through another material bend the light again so it meets in a focused point.

Label the lens. Draw lines to show how light moves through it. Then, describe the movement.

reflecting telescope

The light enters the lens. It changes speed and bends as it moves through a different material. As the light leaves the glass, the angle of the glass and moving through another material bend the light again so it spreads out.

The Hubble Space Telescope orbits above Earth's atmosphere. It is a reflecting telescope that is about the size of a school bus. It senses infrared, ultraviolet, and visible light, taking pictures of the images and sending the information to scientists on Earth.

Light and radiation travel at different speeds through various materials in the atmosphere. They bend as they move through each material, making the image blurry. Telescopes in space will have clearer images because there is nothing to move through.

Day #1 / Day #2 / Day #3 / Day #4

Name
Week # 27: Telescopes

Assessment # 27

Read the paragraph. Then, answer the questions.

Galileo did not build the first refracting telescope, but he improved it. Experimenting with convex lens, he was the first person to clearly view craters on Earth's moon. Another great scientist, Sir Isaac Newton, experimented with light. He found that using a concave mirror, flat mirror, and a convex lens made the heavenly views clearer and closer. His telescope became known as the reflecting telescope.

1. Think about the names of the two telescopes. How does each use light?

The refracting telescope bends light to a point to focus images. The reflecting telescope bends light out to focus images.

2. Choose one scientist mentioned in the paragraph. Give two reasons why he was a good scientist.

Answers will vary.

3. Why do scientists want to study space?

Answers will vary.

Fill in the circle next to the best answer.

4. Why does a radio telescope have a reflector that is shaped like a dish?
   - (A) It spreads out the waves so the antenna can read them.
   - ● It catches the waves and focuses them on the antenna.
   - (C) It focuses the waves to a point on the lens.
   - (D) It spreads out the waves so the lens can collect the light.

Name
Week # 28: Satellites

Possible answer: They are alike because both orbit another object. They are different because a natural satellite is a body made in nature. A human-made one is made with parts constructed by people.

Possible answers: The moon and Earth are natural satellites. The space station and weather satellites are human-made.

What is the purpose of a scientific satellite?

Possible answer: They collect data about changes on Earth.

How would this satellite help scientists?

Answers will vary.

List three conditions a weather satellite tracks.

Possible answers: They collect cloud cover, atmospheric pressure, and wind flow.

How does the information from a weather satellite help people on Earth?

Answers will vary.

What kind of satellite does a cell phone need?

Cell phones need a communication satellite.

What would your life be like without this satellite?

Answers will vary.

Day #1 / Day #2 / Day #3 / Day #4

Name
Week # 28: Satellites

Assessment # 28

Answer the questions.

1. Some governments launch military satellites to track the movements of people, vehicles, and missiles in other countries. Do you think this is a good idea? Write a paragraph that explains your opinion and if it is a morally responsible practice.

Answers will vary.

2. What happens to a satellite that stops working or is no longer needed?

Scientists will try to repair it, either through computer programs or with astronaut help. If it cannot be fixed or is not useful, scientists will turn it off. Eventually, the satellite will stop moving, fall, and burn up in Earth's atmosphere.

3. Think about the many different satellites and their uses. Which do you think impacts your life the most? Why?

Answers will vary.

Fill in the circle next to the best answer.

4. Which kind of satellite would a global positioning system (GPS) use?
   - ● navigation
   - (B) military
   - (C) communication
   - (D) scientific

Answer Key

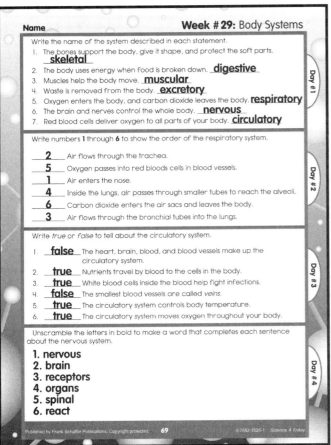

Week #29: Body Systems

Name

Write the name of the system described in each statement.

Day #1

1. The bones support the body, give it shape, and protect the soft parts.
   __skeletal__
2. The body uses energy when food is broken down. __digestive__
3. Muscles help the body move. __muscular__
4. Waste is removed from the body. __excretory__
5. Oxygen enters the body, and carbon dioxide leaves the body. __respiratory__
6. The brain and nerves control the whole body. __nervous__
7. Red blood cells deliver oxygen to all parts of your body. __circulatory__

Write numbers **1** through **6** to show the order of the respiratory system.

Day #2

- __2__ Air flows through the trachea.
- __5__ Oxygen passes into red bloods cells in blood vessels.
- __1__ Air enters the nose.
- __4__ Inside the lungs, air passes through smaller tubes to reach the alveoli.
- __6__ Carbon dioxide enters the air sacs and leaves the body.
- __3__ Air flows through the bronchial tubes into the lungs.

Write *true* or *false* to tell about the circulatory system.

Day #3

1. __false__ The heart, brain, blood, and blood vessels make up the circulatory system.
2. __true__ Nutrients travel by blood to the cells in the body.
3. __true__ White blood cells inside the blood help fight infections.
4. __false__ The smallest blood vessels are called *veins*.
5. __true__ The circulatory system controls body temperature.
6. __true__ The circulatory system moves oxygen throughout your body.

Unscramble the letters in bold to make a word that completes each sentence about the nervous system.

Day #4

1. nervous
2. brain
3. receptors
4. organs
5. spinal
6. react

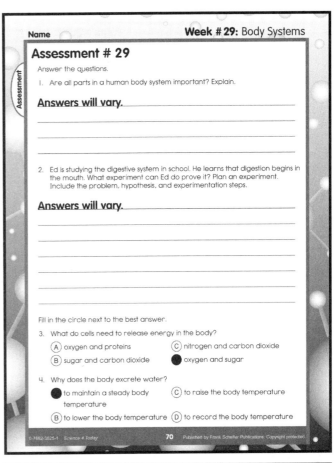

Week #29: Body Systems

Name

Assessment # 29

Answer the questions.

1. Are all parts in a human body system important? Explain.

   __Answers will vary.__

2. Ed is studying the digestive system in school. He learns that digestion begins in the mouth. What experiment can Ed do prove it? Plan an experiment. Include the problem, hypothesis, and experimentation steps.

   __Answers will vary.__

Fill in the circle next to the best answer.

3. What do cells need to release energy in the body?
   - (A) oxygen and proteins
   - (B) sugar and carbon dioxide
   - (C) nitrogen and carbon dioxide
   - ● oxygen and sugar

4. Why does the body excrete water?
   - ● to maintain a steady body temperature
   - (B) to lower the body temperature
   - (C) to raise the body temperature
   - (D) to record the body temperature

Week #30: Healthy Lifestyles

Name

Day #1

A healthy diet provides the nutrients that give the body energy. It helps keep people from injury and illness.

Each color of food has different minerals and nutrients. Eating from all the colors makes sure that the body is getting a variety of minerals and nutrients for better nutrition.

Day #2

Possible answers: Exercise keeps the muscles strong. It builds the muscles and lungs so that the heart can pump more blood and the lungs can get more air. Exercise can reduce stress for better mental health. It helps people sleep better, too.

Answers will vary.

Day #3

What is hygiene?

Hygiene is the practice of keeping the body clean to stay healthy.

What are three good hygiene practices you follow?

Answers will vary.

Day #4

Draw a line to match each word with its definition.

drugs — chemicals that change the way the body works
prescription drugs — chemicals that a person can buy in a store
illegal drugs — using drugs for reasons other than health
dependence — a mental or physical need to use a drug
nicotine — a chemical in cigarettes that makes the heart beat faster
alcohol — a liquid chemical that slows the brain
drug abuse — chemicals that are not allowed by law

Week #30: Healthy Lifestyles

Name

Assessment # 30

1. Why is it important to warm up and cool down before exercising?

   Possible answer: Warming up stretches the muscles to prevent injury, and cooling down prevents muscle soreness.

2. Why are safety rules important? Include three examples of rules you follow in your explanation.

   __Answers will vary.__

3. A friend begins smoking a cigarette. What will you say and do?

   __Answers will vary.__

Fill in the circle next to the best answer.

4. Which is not a nutrient your body needs?
   - (A) proteins
   - (B) carbohydrates
   - ● sugars
   - (D) fats

5. To which drug can people form a dependence?
   - (A) alcohol
   - (B) nicotine
   - (C) marijuana
   - ● all of the above

Answer Key

Name

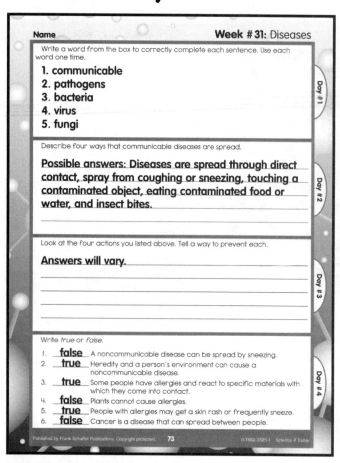

Week # 31: Diseases

Write a word from the box to correctly complete each sentence. Use each word one time.

1. communicable
2. pathogens
3. bacteria
4. virus
5. fungi

Day #1

Describe four ways that communicable diseases are spread.

Possible answers: Diseases are spread through direct contact, spray from coughing or sneezing, touching a contaminated object, eating contaminated food or water, and insect bites.

Day #2

Look at the four actions you listed above. Tell a way to prevent each.

Answers will vary.

Day #3

Write *true* or *false*.

1. **false** A noncommunicable disease can be spread by sneezing.
2. **true** Heredity and a person's environment can cause a noncommunicable disease.
3. **true** Some people have allergies and react to specific materials with which they come into contact.
4. **false** Plants cannot cause allergies.
5. **true** People with allergies may get a skin rash or frequently sneeze.
6. **false** Cancer is a disease that can spread between people.

Day #4

Published by Frank Schaffer Publications. Copyright protected. 73   0-7682-3525-1 *Science 4 Today*

Name

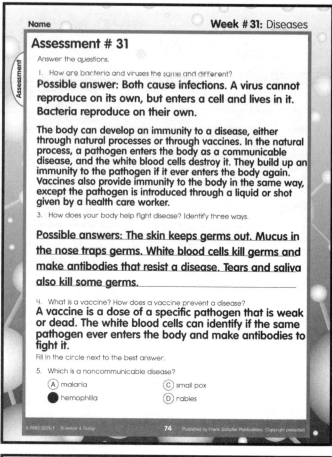

Week # 31: Diseases

Assessment # 31

Answer the questions.

1. How are bacteria and viruses the same and different?

Possible answer: Both cause infections. A virus cannot reproduce on its own, but enters a cell and lives in it. Bacteria reproduce on their own.

The body can develop an immunity to a disease, either through natural processes or through vaccines. In the natural process, a pathogen enters the body as a communicable disease, and the white blood cells destroy it. They build up an immunity to the pathogen if it ever enters the body again. Vaccines also provide immunity to the body in the same way, except the pathogen is introduced through a liquid or shot given by a health care worker.

3. How does your body help fight disease? Identify three ways.

Possible answers: The skin keeps germs out. Mucus in the nose traps germs. White blood cells kill germs and make antibodies that resist a disease. Tears and saliva also kill some germs.

4. What is a vaccine? How does a vaccine prevent a disease?
A vaccine is a dose of a specific pathogen that is weak or dead. The white blood cells can identify if the same pathogen ever enters the body and make antibodies to fight it.

Fill in the circle next to the best answer.

5. Which is a noncommunicable disease?
   - (A) malaria
   - (C) small pox
   - ● hemophilia
   - (D) rabies

0-7682-3525-1 *Science 4 Today*   74   Published by Frank Schaffer Publications. Copyright protected.

Name

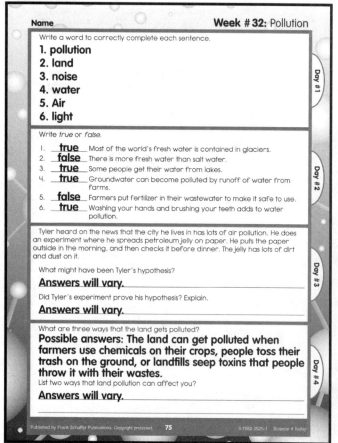

Week # 32: Pollution

Write a word to correctly complete each sentence.

1. pollution
2. land
3. noise
4. water
5. Air
6. light

Day #1

Write *true* or *false*.

1. **true** Most of the world's fresh water is contained in glaciers.
2. **false** There is more fresh water than salt water.
3. **true** Some people get their water from lakes.
4. **true** Groundwater can become polluted by runoff of water from farms.
5. **false** Farmers put fertilizer in their wastewater to make it safe to use.
6. **true** Washing your hands and brushing your teeth adds to water pollution.

Day #2

Tyler heard on the news that the city he lives in has lots of air pollution. He does an experiment where he spreads petroleum jelly on paper. He puts the paper outside in the morning, and then checks it before dinner. The jelly has lots of dirt and dust on it.

What might have been Tyler's hypothesis?
Answers will vary.

Did Tyler's experiment prove his hypothesis? Explain.
Answers will vary.

Day #3

What are three ways that the land gets polluted?
Possible answers: The land can get polluted when farmers use chemicals on their crops, people toss their trash on the ground, or landfills seep toxins that people throw it with their wastes.
List two ways that land pollution can affect you?
Answers will vary.

Day #4

Published by Frank Schaffer Publications. Copyright protected. 75   0-7682-3525-1 *Science 4 Today*

Name

Week # 32: Pollution

Assessment # 32

Answer the questions.

1. Can the music you listen to cause noise pollution? Explain.

Possible answer: Yes, music can cause pollution if it is played very loudly.

2. Which form of pollution is the biggest problem in your community? Identify it, its causes, and its effects. Then, suggest a way tell how to solve the problem.

Answers will vary.

Fill in the circle next to the best answer.

3. Which is not a pollutant?
   - (A) a jack hammer
   - (C) fertilizer
   - (B) volcanic ash
   - ● water

4. What is the main contribution to rising ozone levels?
   - ● burning fossil fuels
   - (C) sunlight
   - (B) space debris
   - (D) tree cutting

0-7682-3525-1 *Science 4 Today*   76   Published by Frank Schaffer Publications. Copyright protected.

Answer Key

Day #1

Possible answers: They construct buildings. They dig minerals from the ground. They build roads.

Possible answers: Buildings provide shelter and places to purchase products. Minerals can be used to make useful products. Roads make it easy to move from place to place.

Day #2

Possible answers: Trees are often cut when building, taking away some of the oxygen-making supply. Minerals are nonrenewable and will someday be used up, which means that some products may not be available anymore. Road construction results in air pollution, with the excess dust and vehicle fumes.

Answers will vary.

Day #3

Possible answer: Ozone gas is a barrier to ultraviolet rays, which can cause cancer.

Possible answer: Fumes from cars and power plants, produced from burning fossil fuels, are destroying the ozone.

The temperature on earth will rise. More people will get cancer.

Day #4

As the human population grew in the United States, people built houses on farmland. This growth caused a decrease in the bluebird population. These birds nested in tree holes they found near open fields. People in some communities began to build special boxes for the birds, placing them in parks and backyards.

Possible answers: People destroyed the bluebirds' habitat, making it impossible for them to find places to nest or food to eat. People helped the population by building places for the birds to nest and kept the birds from becoming extinct.

Assessment

Assessment # 33

Read the paragraph. Then, answer the questions.

Kudzu is a plant indigenous to Japan. It grows quickly and has beautiful, fragrant flowers. People brought it to the United States to help prevent soil erosion, feed animals, and decorate gardens. However, kudzu grew so well in the south, that it totally covered many native flowers, shrubs, and trees, killing the plants. The United States Department of Agriculture declared that kudzu was a weed in 1972 and began killing it. The plant, needing several applications of herbicides, was hard to kill. In the meantime, several people worked to find uses for the plant. They make baskets, jelly, and syrup from kudzu. Preliminary testing also shows that it may one day be made into a useful drug.

1. How did the decision to plant kudzu negatively impact the U.S.?

It killed many trees, shrubs, and flowers.

2. How did the decision positively impact the U.S.?

Possible answer: For a while, kudzu stopped erosion and was used as a food source for some animals. People use it to make useful products.

3. Why did people change their view of kudzu?

People changed their views because it began killing the native plants.

4. Is kudzu a resource? Explain.

Yes, kudzu is a resource because people have found ways to make it into products that people use.

5. Why did the native plants die?

The plants died because they lacked sunlight to allow photosynthesis to make the food they needed to live.

Day #1

Which kind of trash is thrown out the most?

Paper is the thrown out the most.

What are three specific kinds of this trash that you throw out at school or home?

Possible answers: Newspaper, notebook paper, packaging materials are paper products.

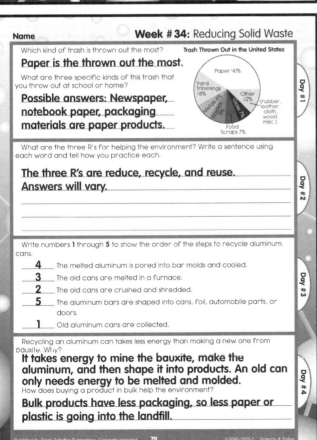

Trash Thrown Out in the United States

Paper 40%
Yard Trimmings 18%
Metals 8%
Glass 7%
Food Scraps 7%
Other 12% (rubber, leather, cloth, wood, misc.)

Day #2

What are the three R's for helping the environment? Write a sentence using each word and tell how you practice each.

The three R's are reduce, recycle, and reuse. Answers will vary.

Day #3

Write numbers **1** through **5** to show the order of the steps to recycle aluminum cans.

__4__ The melted aluminum is pored into bar molds and cooled.

__3__ The old cans are melted in a furnace.

__2__ The old cans are crushed and shredded.

__5__ The aluminum bars are shaped into cans, foil, automobile parts, or doors.

__1__ Old aluminum cans are collected.

Day #4

Recycling an aluminum can takes less energy than making a new one from bauxite. Why?

It takes energy to mine the bauxite, make the aluminum, and then shape it into products. An old can only needs energy to be melted and molded.

How does buying a product in bulk help the environment?

Bulk products have less packaging, so less paper or plastic is going into the landfill.

Assessment

Assessment # 34

Answer the questions.

1. How does reducing solid waste help Earth? Explain three ways.

Reducing solid wastes protects Earth because it keeps landfills from growing too rapidly, it conserves nonrenewable natural resources, and it protects the air from pollution when companies make products.

2. What might happen to Earth if people do not reduce solid wastes? List three effects.

Possible answer: There will not be enough land for landfills. Natural resources will run out more quickly. The land will continue to be more polluted.

3. Yard clippings, orange peels, coffee grounds, and other food scraps can be put into a mulch pile. Explain what a mulch pile is, how it works, and what it can be used for. Use the words in the box in your explanation.

| energy | nutrients | decomposers | decay |

Possible answer: A mulch pile is made of food scraps, yard clippings, and other organic materials that rot and decay. Worms, maggots, bacteria, and other decomposers work to release the stored energy from these materials so that the nutrients can be returned to the soil to aid plant growth when spread as a blanket on the ground.

Fill in the circle next to the best answer.

4. Which product is made from recycled rubber?

● running tracks   Ⓒ coffee mugs

Ⓑ playground slides   Ⓓ windows

Answer Key

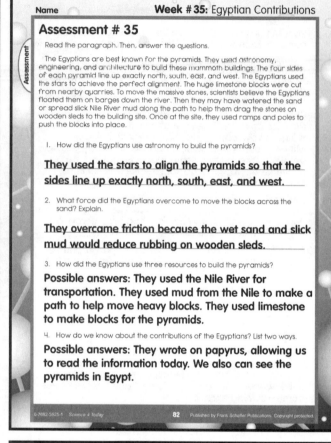

Week # 35: Egyptian Contributions

The ancient Egyptians spent much time looking up at the sky and made two basic discoveries that affect our daily life. First, they gave us the measurement of time in the form of a 24-hour day. They also fixed the year to include 365 days.

What two cycles did the Egyptians use to help them measure time? Explain.

Possible answers: They used the sun and stars to measure time.

Day #1

Hygiene was important to the Egyptians. Water was in great supply, so they washed often. They reduced odors by placing small balls of incense and porridge where body limbs met. The people chewed herbs and used milk as a gargle to make the breath smell better. Wealthy women used cleansing cream made of oil and lime.

What products do you use today that are like the ones used by Egyptians?

People use deodorants under their arms to reduce odors, mouthwash and toothpaste to clean their mouths, and soap for washing their faces.

Day #2

The ancient Egyptians are also one of the earliest civilizations to use make-up. They lined their eyes with green malachite or black kohl. They ground colored minerals and mixed them with water to make a paste to apply to the eyelid. They combined fat and other red minerals to make lip color. Finally, red ochre and fat

Possible answer: The make-up is the same because the products are applied to the eyes, cheeks, and lips. They are different the Egyptians used natural resources to make their colors. Most products today have dyes in them.

Day #3

Information written on papyrus tell how early Egyptian doctors used the plants around them as medicines. They used onions to prevent colds and thyme as a pain reliever. Aloe vera was used to treat headaches, burns, and skin diseases. They used honey for a number of illnesses, from sore throats to antibiotics to spread on wounds.

Why were the early doctors good scientists?

Possible answer: Yes, they were good scientists because they communicated the ingredients they used in their medicines.

Day #4

Week # 35: Egyptian Contributions

Assessment # 35

Read the paragraph. Then, answer the questions.

The Egyptians are best known for the pyramids. They used astronomy, engineering, and architecture to build these mammoth buildings. The four sides of each pyramid line up exactly north, south, east, and west. The Egyptians used the stars to achieve the perfect alignment. The huge limestone blocks were cut from nearby quarries. To move the massive stones, scientists believe the Egyptians floated them on barges down the river. Then they may have watered the sand or spread slick Nile River mud along the path to help them drag the stones on wooden sleds to the building site. Once at the site, they used ramps and poles to push the blocks into place.

1. How did the Egyptians use astronomy to build the pyramids?

They used the stars to align the pyramids so that the sides line up exactly north, south, east, and west.

2. What force did the Egyptians overcome to move the blocks across the sand? Explain.

They overcame friction because the wet sand and slick mud would reduce rubbing on wooden sleds.

3. How did the Egyptians use three resources to build the pyramids?

Possible answers: They used the Nile River for transportation. They used mud from the Nile to make a path to help move heavy blocks. They used limestone to make blocks for the pyramids.

4. How do we know about the contributions of the Egyptians? List two ways.

Possible answers: They wrote on papyrus, allowing us to read the information today. We also can see the pyramids in Egypt.

Assessment

Week #36: The History of the Automobile

In the late 1700s, people began using steam as a source of energy in manufacturing. Nicolas-Joseph Cugnot thought that it would be a possible to use the steam engine for transportation. From 1769 to 1770, he built two self-propelled, steam-powered vehicles. One carried passengers, and the other was a tractor to move war supplies. The vehicles blew huge clouds of steam into the air, and they required a lot of work to keep the steam pressure up.

How did the steam engine create energy?

Water was heated and turned into steam. The pressure of the trapped steam created energy.

Day #1

The modern car did not develop until the invention of the internal combustion engine. In 1860, Jean Lenoir invented an engine where coal gas exploded to make an energy source. In 1863, using petroleum as the fuel, he built the engine in a wagon and drove it 50 miles.

Even though Lenoir had an engine that worked, why do you think that he kept trying to improve it?

Answers will vary.

Day #2

The first electric car was built in 1891. It ran on batteries and could carry six passengers. The cars became very popular because they were quiet, lacked the smoke and fumes of the steam-powered cars, and were easily operated. However, the batteries allowed the car to only go about 50 miles before being recharged, and they did not go very fast.

Possible answers: They were alike because both vehicles could carry passengers. They were different because one used steam as a power source and the other used batteries.

Day #3

Possible answer: The conveyor belt automatically moved cars mechanically along a path so that workers could add their parts in a short period of time. The process made it possible to manufacture cars more quickly to meet the demand. Because they did it so quickly, the cost was cheaper as well.

Day #4

Week #36: The History of the Automobile

Assessment # 36

1. Use the information from the week to complete a timeline to show the history of the automobile. **Answers will vary:**

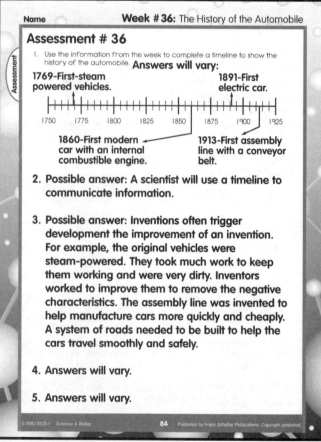

1769-First-steam powered vehicles.

1891-First electric car.

1750 1775 1800 1825 1850 1875 1900 1925

1860-First modern car with an internal combustible engine.

1913-First assembly line with a conveyor belt.

2. **Possible answer: A scientist will use a timeline to communicate information.**

3. **Possible answer: Inventions often trigger development the improvement of an invention. For example, the original vehicles were steam-powered. They took much work to keep them working and were very dirty. Inventors worked to improve them to remove the negative characteristics. The assembly line was invented to help manufacture cars more quickly and cheaply. A system of roads needed to be built to help the cars travel smoothly and safely.**

4. **Answers will vary.**

5. **Answers will vary.**

Assessment

Answer Key

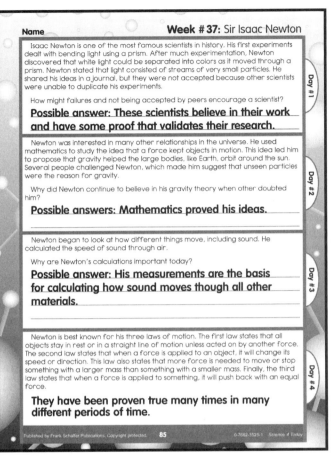

Name

Week #37: Sir Isaac Newton

Isaac Newton is one of the most famous scientists in history. His first experiments dealt with bending light using a prism. After much experimentation, Newton discovered that white light could be separated into colors as it moved through a prism. Newton stated that light consisted of streams of very small particles. He shared his ideas in a journal, but they were not accepted because other scientists were unable to duplicate his experiments.

Day #1

How might failures and not being accepted by peers encourage a scientist?

Possible answer: These scientists believe in their work and have some proof that validates their research.

Newton was interested in many other relationships in the universe. He used mathematics to study the idea that a force kept objects in motion. This idea led him to propose that gravity helped the large bodies, like Earth, orbit around the sun. Several people challenged Newton, which made him suggest that unseen particles were the reason for gravity.

Day #2

Why did Newton continue to believe in his gravity theory when other doubted him?

Possible answers: Mathematics proved his ideas.

Newton began to look at how different things move, including sound. He calculated the speed of sound through air.

Day #3

Why are Newton's calculations important today?

Possible answer: His measurements are the basis for calculating how sound moves though all other materials.

Newton is best known for his three laws of motion. The first law states that all objects stay in rest or in a straight line of motion unless acted on by another force. The second law states that when a force is applied to an object, it will change its speed or direction. This law also states that more force is needed to move or stop something with a larger mass than something with a smaller mass. Finally, the third law states that when a force is applied to something, it will push back with an equal force.

Day #4

They have been proven true many times in many different periods of time.

Published by Frank Schaffer Publications. Copyright protected. 85   0-7682-3525-1 *Science 4 Today*

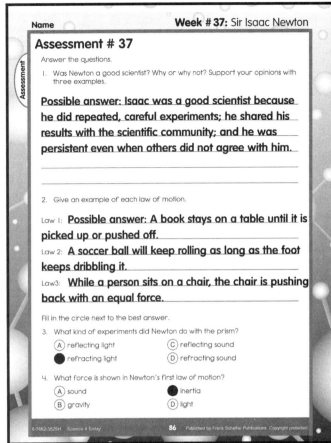

Name

Week #37: Sir Isaac Newton

Assessment

Assessment # 37

Answer the questions.

1. Was Newton a good scientist? Why or why not? Support your opinions with three examples.

Possible answer: Isaac was a good scientist because he did repeated, careful experiments; he shared his results with the scientific community; and he was persistent even when others did not agree with him.

2. Give an example of each law of motion.

Law 1: **Possible answer: A book stays on a table until it is picked up or pushed off.**

Law 2: **A soccer ball will keep rolling as long as the foot keeps dribbling it.**

Law 3: **While a person sits on a chair, the chair is pushing back with an equal force.**

Fill in the circle next to the best answer.

3. What kind of experiments did Newton do with the prism?
   - (A) reflecting light
   - ● refracting light
   - (C) reflecting sound
   - (D) refracting sound

4. What force is shown in Newton's first law of motion?
   - (A) sound
   - (B) gravity
   - ● inertia
   - (D) light

0-7682-3525-1 *Science 4 Today*   86 Published by Frank Schaffer Publications. Copyright protected.

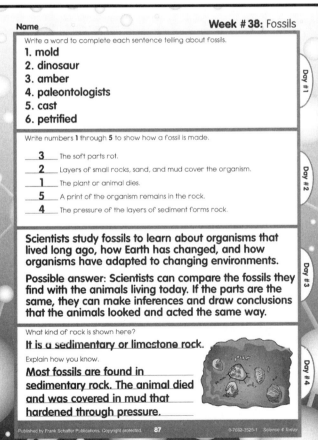

Name

Week #38: Fossils

Write a word to complete each sentence telling about fossils.

Day #1

1. mold
2. dinosaur
3. amber
4. paleontologists
5. cast
6. petrified

Write numbers **1** through **5** to show how a fossil is made.

Day #2

- **3** The soft parts rot.
- **2** Layers of small rocks, sand, and mud cover the organism.
- **1** The plant or animal dies.
- **5** A print of the organism remains in the rock.
- **4** The pressure of the layers of sediment forms rock.

Scientists study fossils to learn about organisms that lived long ago, how Earth has changed, and how organisms have adapted to changing environments.

Day #3

Possible answer: Scientists can compare the fossils they find with the animals living today. If the parts are the same, they can make inferences and draw conclusions that the animals looked and acted the same way.

What kind of rock is shown here?

It is a sedimentary or limestone rock.

Day #4

Explain how you know.

Most fossils are found in sedimentary rock. The animal died and was covered in mud that hardened through pressure.

Published by Frank Schaffer Publications. Copyright protected. 87   0-7682-3525-1 *Science 4 Today*

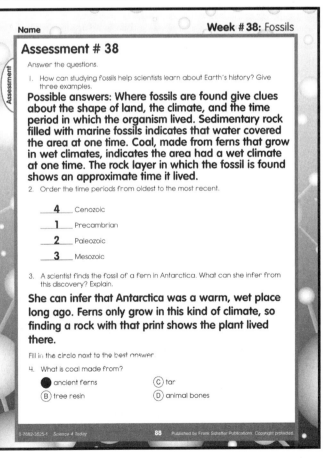

Name

Week #38: Fossils

Assessment

Assessment # 38

Answer the questions.

1. How can studying fossils help scientists learn about Earth's history? Give three examples.

Possible answers: Where fossils are found give clues about the shape of land, the climate, and the time period in which the organism lived. Sedimentary rock filled with marine fossils indicates that water covered the area at one time. Coal, made from ferns that grow in wet climates, indicates the area had a wet climate at one time. The rock layer in which the fossil is found shows an approximate time it lived.

2. Order the time periods from oldest to the most recent.

   - **4** Cenozoic
   - **1** Precambrian
   - **2** Paleozoic
   - **3** Mesozoic

3. A scientist finds the fossil of a fern in Antarctica. What can she infer from this discovery? Explain.

She can infer that Antarctica was a warm, wet place long ago. Ferns only grow in this kind of climate, so finding a rock with that print shows the plant lived there.

Fill in the circle next to the best answer.

4. What is coal made from?
   - ● ancient ferns
   - (B) tree resin
   - (C) tar
   - (D) animal bones

0-7682-3525-1 *Science 4 Today*   88 Published by Frank Schaffer Publications. Copyright protected.

Answer Key

Name

Week #39: Cycles in Nature

Unscramble the letters in bold print to make a word that names a cycle.

1. lunar
2. life
3. oxygen
4. photosynthesis
5. seasonal
6. water

Day #1

Write *true* or *false*.

1. **false** The amount of nitrogen changes because of the nitrogen cycle.
2. **true** The proteins in nitrogen promote cell growth and repair.
3. **true** Most organisms cannot use nitrogen gas.
4. **false** Lightning and special kinds of bacteria turn nitrogen compounds into gas.
5. **true** Decomposers restore nitrogen to soil.
6. **true** Nitrogen made by lightning washes into the soil with the help of rain.

Day #2

Draw a line to match each phase with its description. Then, write numbers **1** through **8** to show the correct order of the lunar cycle.

4 waxing gibbous moon — The moon looks like a big, bright circle.
7 third-quarter moon — A sliver of the shrinking moon is lit.
6 waning gibbous moon — A sliver of the growing moon is lit.
2 waxing crescent moon — One half of the shrinking moon is lit.
3 first-quarter moon — The moon looks dark in the night sky.
8 waning crescent moon — The growing moon's surface is mostly lit.
1 new moon — One half of the growing moon is lit.
5 full moon — The shrinking moon's surface is mostly lit.

Day #3

Seeds germinate in the soil when a root begins to grow down and the stem begins to grow up. Next, the leaves and stem grow above the soil to make a seedling. The mature plant produces flowers. Wind, birds, bees, or other insects pollinate the flowers. The pollen grains join with eggs. Seeds form and scatter on the ground when the flower dies.

Day #4

Name

Week #39: Cycles in Nature

Assessment

Assessment # 39

Fill in the circle next to the best answer.

1. Which is not a factor in the rock cycle?
   - (A) heat
   - ● air
   - (B) pressure
   - (D) erosion

2. Which force affects tides?
   - (A) friction
   - (C) inertia
   - ● gravity
   - (D) magnetism

3. Which form of energy causes the water cycle?
   - (A) static electricity
   - (C) infrared
   - ● solar
   - (D) sound

4. Ito sees this flowering plant in the garden. What part of the life cycle does he see?

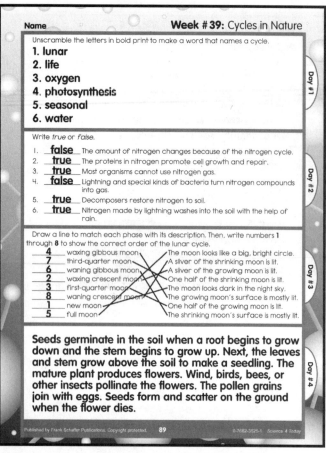

   - ● seedling
   - (C) germinating
   - (B) seed
   - (D) pollinating

Answer the question.

5. Many cycles are interrelated. For one cycle to continue, it needs the help of another. Choose two cycles. Tell how they work together. Then, explain why they are important to the balance of nature.

Answers will vary. _____

_____

_____

_____

Name

Week #40: Kid Inventors

What do people invent things? Give two reasons.

Possible answers: People invent things to solve a problem or because they have an idea for a product or process.

Name one inventor. Tell what the person invented and why it was useful.

Answers will vary. _____

_____

Day #1

At the age of nine, Brandon Whale visited the hospital and saw young children crying when they got shots. Whale discovered that the children's veins were small and hard to locate. Moreover, the veins were even harder to find when the children were anxious and tense. Whale made a soft ball that looked like a beetle. Children could squeeze it, which helped the veins relax. The kids relaxed, too, because they liked to hold the toy. Brandon called his invention the "Needle Beetle." A toy company liked the idea so much that they started to manufacture Whale's invention.

Why did Whale invent the "Needle Beetle"?

Whale saw a problem that needed to be solved.

Day #2

At the age of eleven, Cassidy Goldstein was doing a school assignment. Many of the crayons she had were broken, so drawing was hard. Goldstein came up with a solution that would hold the broken crayons. Goldstein, using the plastic tube that held water for a single rose, put the crayon in the tube. The holder worked much like a teacher's chalk holder. It was an instant success with the teacher for two reasons. It made small pieces of crayons useable, and children could more easily grip the broken crayons.

It made broken crayons easier to use, and it could help small children, who did not have good motor control, draw.

Day #3

With the help of her father, Cassidy Goldstein patented the "Crayon Holder," which meant that she would keep the right to build and sell the invention. Goldstein now sells the holder through catalogs and in some major stores. Moreover, Goldstein's invention gave her father an idea, too. Mr. Goldstein formed a company that helps kids build, market, and sell their inventions.

Goldstein's father got a new idea from his experiences helping his daughter. He thought there might be other kids like Cassidy who had good ideas, but because of their age, they would not be able to build and sell them.

Day #4

Name

Week #40: Kid Inventors

Assessment

Assessment # 40

Fill in the circle next to the best answer.

1. Which could be Brandon Whale's hypothesis for making the Needle Beetle?
   - (A) Beetles are cute.
   - ● Children will feel less anxious about shots if they hold something cute.
   - (C) Squeezing something makes the veins bigger.
   - (D) Crying children are unhappy.

2. Which is a characteristic of a good inventor?
   - ● observant
   - (C) quick
   - (B) happy
   - (D) selfish

Answer the questions.

3. Is an inventor a scientist? Explain.

Answers will vary. _____

_____

_____

4. Many inventions are made to solve a problem. Think of a problem you would like to solve. Design an invention for it. Explain the invention below and tell how it solves the problem.

Answers will vary. _____

_____

_____

_____

_____
